On the Scent of Danger

On the Scent of Danger

PHYLLIS ROSSITER

AVALON BOOKS
THOMAS BOUREGY AND COMPANY, INC.
401 LAFAYETTE STREET
NEW YORK, NEW YORK 10003

PRINTED IN THE UNITED STATES OF AMERICA
BY HADDON CRAFTSMEN, SCRANTON, PENNSYLVANIA

To my friend Joan Johnson

And to all the other concerned, courageous
bloodhound trainers and handlers—and to all
the real "Cosmos" and "Moonshines"

Chapter One

*I*t was snowing harder, and Police Officer Lucky McCall could barely see a foot ahead of her. Wet branches slapped her face as she pounded through them. Cosmo, her bloodhound, lunged ahead and threw his weight into the harness, threatening to pull her off her feet if she couldn't keep up. Her shoulders ached.

The bloodhound's panting rasped, and his tail wagged faster and faster. Recognizing his end-of-the-trail excitement, Lucky tightened her hold on the knots in the nylon lead. In his frenzy to finally reach their quarry, her control over him would become less firm. They must be very near the old woman who had wandered off from the nursing home.

Lucky swiped at her face with her free hand. Rather than drifting down in flakes, the snow pelted her with heavy wet fistfuls—Old Man Winter's last tantrum before yielding to spring, the kind of unexpected and treacherous late storm that

1

Grandpa called a "blackbird storm," a spell of blustery weather after the blackbirds had returned.

She glanced over her shoulder. Either her new backup had fallen even farther behind or else the visibility was so bad she couldn't see him. Judging by his complaints the last time she'd heard from him, he might even have given up the chase. Big deal. She didn't need him anyway.

Her windbreaker was as soaked as the rest of her uniform, and the gloved fingers clutching the dog's lead were nearly numb. Somewhere on the track behind them a branch had clawed off her stocking cap. Her wet ponytail clung to her face and she wished she had taken the time to braid it.

But the old woman was probably worse off. Lucky ignored the nagging stitch in her side and extended her stride. With his great head held high, Cosmo was now air-scenting the fresh and unmistakable trail.

She peered into the swirling snow. Soon now. But would it be soon enough? She hated an end of the trail when they were too late. Poor Cosmo. She knew he felt the same urgency to reach the woman in time.

From far off, Lucky heard the honk of a car horn. Probably she could hear additional traffic if she had time to listen. Though she had encountered them many times, these pockets of dense woods in the heart of the suburbs always surprised her. One could die of exposure here just as easily as in an

Ozark forest. She couldn't understand how a nursing home could just let someone wander off into the cold, and probably without a coat. With darkness coming on, Cosmo had better find the old woman soon.

Suddenly a high, thin keening floated on the snow. Lucky shivered, but couldn't be sure she hadn't imagined the sound under their crashing progress, her thudding footfalls, the dog's labored breathing, and her pulse pounding in her ears. She held her breath and strained to listen.

Somebody was singing. Was it the old woman? Cosmo bounded forward, dragging her after him, forcing her to run to stay on her feet. On the wind was the eerie rise and fall of the woman's song, and then insane laughter like a witch's cackle. But Lucky couldn't be sure where it came from.

Cosmo knew, though, and he surged through the underbrush.

And then a new sound—the unmistakable rumble of a train. Lucky gasped as the ground trembled beneath her feet. They must be very near the tracks. The diesel's warning blasted her ears. *We must be right on top of it,* she thought.

Where was the old woman? Did she hear the train? Was she so confused or senile that she might wander into its path?

"Stay where you are!" Lucky shouted. "Please stay put! Don't move!" Even as she called out, she knew there was little chance the woman could hear her over the obliterating noise of the train. They must find her *now.*

She dashed the snowflakes from her eyelashes and tried to penetrate the veil as she ran. She couldn't see the train, but she heard clearly the squeaks and rattles of its passing, and it was dangerously close.

"Cosmo, stay!" she shouted. Better to stop and reconnoiter. Better a brief pause. They couldn't help the old woman if they stumbled onto the tracks.

But Cosmo did not stop. Either he couldn't hear her voice over the thunderous train or else, in his eagerness to reach the imminent end of his trail, he chose to ignore the command.

Lucky hauled on the dog's lead with both hands, attempting to plant her feet and dig in with her heels. But she knew she'd never stop him physically. *He's more than a hundred pounds of charging bloodhound,* she reminded herself. *I might as well try to stop the train.* "Stay, Cosmo!" she cried.

The bloodhound hesitated and flung her a glance over his shoulder. His wrinkled brow gave him a worried look. *Not now,* his eyes seemed to plead. *We're so close, so very close.* He never broke his stride. Her command to "find!" overrode all else; he was determined to drop dead in his tracks before he'd leave a trail unrun, his quarry unfound.

The ground lifted beneath Lucky's feet, and then just as suddenly fell away. Head down, nose to the trail, Cosmo had hurtled over a slight rise and towed her after him down the steep pitch of a hill. *No! The embankment, the railroad embankment!* They rushed straight for the tracks. A blur of motion and sound told Lucky that the train was roaring by just below them.

She threw herself backward and leaned against Cosmo's lead with all her might. Loose soil, muddied by the wet snow, slid under her heels; stones loosened by their passing rolled beside her and bounced into the roadbed. Her feet slid out from under her, and she fell heavily, clinging desperately to the hound's lead with one hand, protecting her face from the stinging brush with the other.

Oblivious to her plight, slowed but not stopped by the dead weight on the lead, Cosmo raced on, his compulsive mission nearing its end.

Lucky clutched at the punishing branches, but not one was big enough to hold her and stop the dog, or sturdy enough to serve as a hitch for the lead. She had no time to gauge the nearness of the train, but she felt on her wet face the breeze of its passing, and its power beat in her temples. If she didn't release the lead, Cosmo would pull her into the train after him. If she did let him go to save herself, he would hurtle to instant death. "Cosmo, halt! Down!" she screamed. "Down, Cosmo!"

She felt the lead slacken a bit, and struggling to free her hand, she remembered how carefully and tightly she had wrapped the line around the palm to secure her hold on the overenthusiastic young dog. "Down, Cosmo!"

The lead went slack, and Lucky caught a glimpse of Cosmo lowering himself to the ground, looking back at her accusingly, puzzled at her change of command. Never before had anything come between them and the quarry. Lucky's slide down the muddy embankment continued unchecked, but she rolled to rest near the bloodhound, only a foot from the track. The train swayed slightly on the rails as it sped past.

"Good dog!" Lucky cried, wrapping her arms around the dog's thick neck and shaking the loose skin there from side to side. "Oh, good boy, Cosmo!" She buried her face against his side and gripped him fiercely.

His body quivered from the anguish of a job undone, the torment of having to obey her when his training and instincts called him on to the end of the trail. His sides heaved as he panted. In moments the snow had whitened his back.

Tears slid down Lucky's cold cheeks and her heart felt full to bursting with gratitude and admiration for the bloodhound. Thank God for all those months of obedience training. Other handlers thought that obedience work was useless for bloodhounds, but she believed differently. Cosmo's training had just saved their lives.

When the train passed at last, Lucky struggled stiffly to her knees. They still had a job to do.

Cosmo watched her expectantly, muscles bunched, ready to spring to his feet at her command. She wrapped the lead around her palm. "Okay, boy, let's go!" She took a deep breath and braced herself for Cosmo's lunge.

The dog sprang to his feet with agility belying his bulk. He sniffed along the steel rail briefly to pick up the scent scattered by the passing of the train, and then he found the old woman's trail and bounded across the tracks.

Lucky stumbled after him. "Good boy, Cosmo!" she cried.

Getting up the other side of the embankment proved as difficult as coming down had been. Cosmo clawed upward only to slide back in the mud and snow. Lucky hesitated. It would do no good for her to go ahead; she could scarcely haul the heavy dog up bodily. Besides, her own footing would be as precarious as his. And if she did precede him up the hill, they might miss the old woman.

With a new burst of energy, Cosmo floundered upward in a frenzy of excitement, and halfway up, he threw her a look over his shoulder and snuffled his lips in triumph. The lead went slack.

Lucky strained to see through the snow and the gathering darkness. The dog nuzzled a snowy mound. Hand over hand on the lead, she hauled herself up to stand at his side.

Heart pounding, Lucky bent over the form beneath the dog's great head. Gently she turned the woman onto her back and felt for the artery in her neck. The pulse was weak, but she was still alive. Climbing out of the railroad cut had been too much for her and she had collapsed. She wore no coat, but Lucky doubted that her own wet windbreaker would be much help. It was time to call for reinforcements.

"Good dog, Cosmo! Good boy!" She fell to her knees beside the dog and hugged him. "You great, big, old hero. Good boy."

Cosmo gave her a thump and a wet kiss, then settled to his belly in the snow. His tongue hung loosely and he panted hard. Now and again he nosed the form beside him and whimpered.

Lucky's stiff fingers fumbled at the radio strapped to her side.

"That's okay, Officer McCall," said a shadow taking shape out of the snow below her. "I'll get it."

She glanced at her backup and nodded. "She's still alive, but I don't know for how long. Tell them to hurry." She crouched beside the woman and tried to shield her from the snow. Cosmo huddled close, and she pulled him to her. If it hadn't been for the bloodhound, the woman would have been dead for sure. The searchers might have combed these woods in the snow all night and passed within a foot of her without knowing it.

Lucky sighed. And just as surely, Cosmo would

never get the credit he deserved. If, by chance, there should be a newspaper account of his exploits, he would probably be described as a German shepherd.

"We're about a mile up the tracks north of the highway," she heard her backup say into his radio. "Be sure they bring blankets. And hurry."

Two hours later, to Lucky's dismay, her knees still felt rubbery as she walked through a narrow maze of dirty walls flaking salmon-colored paint. Their suburban police station had suffered from the deep budget cuts of recent years, but the handcuffs were still hooked to the chest-high reception counter, the Breathalyzer still worked hard, and Wanted posters still served as decoration. The dark hallway leading to her sergeant's office had never seemed longer.

Her backup was already there, bent over his paperwork. "Hey, Lucille, way to go," he tossed at her as she entered the room. Coming from a male officer, it was close to praise.

"Thanks," she said, careful to meet his eyes, and wondering whether to smile. She allowed herself a slight grin. "But Cosmo deserves the credit," she added. "And please, call me Lucky."

Her sergeant looked up from his desk and snapped, "You're late, McCall. That report is overdue." His granite face never changed expression, but his eyes flickered over her. The badge centered precisely on his perfectly pressed shirt was polished to a dazzle.

Lucky nodded. "I had a dog to take care of." Though she had expected no hero's welcome for simply doing her job, she would have appreciated even a curt "well done."

She adjusted her tie and wished she had taken time to change; the extra uniform in her locker was for just such occasions. Ordinarily she was proud of her uniformed appearance. The pastel-blue shirt over navy trousers accentuated and highlighted the blue of her eyes. But her encounter with the railroad embankment had left her less than regulation neat.

Assembling the necessary forms to be completed, she sat down across from the other officer. The holster of her side arm clunked against the table. In her weariness she had forgotten her firm resolve to handle her weapon "more professionally," as the sergeant often reminded her. A glance his way confirmed that he had noticed. And that he still thought that a woman had no business being a cop.

Lucky sighed; most of the time she didn't feel much like a cop. Whether he thought he was keeping her out of the way or out of danger, the sergeant refused to give her a criminal case. She wondered if she should talk to him again. If she were a man, the sergeant could not justify this steady run of "shopping center" jobs. But, of course, it was important work, which was why she had put up with the discrimination of the sergeant and a few other officers.

And, of course, the bloodhounds earned their keep when, as tonight, they saved a life. But while she and her dogs had an impressive record of finds—lost toddlers and oldsters, mental patients who had wandered off, drowning victims, and so on—the Kansas City, Missouri, Police Department, in the person of this sergeant, had never seen fit to use them to pursue a criminal. And she had never really been able to prove that she was as good a cop as her father. Or any other man. *Even to myself,* she thought.

She half turned in her chair. Now might be as good a time as any to remind the sergeant—one more time—that she was an equal member of this police force. After tonight's successful trail he might listen more attentively. But on the other hand, he might use it as ammunition to prove that she was needed solely to find missing persons. She hesitated.

The sergeant's phone rang and he snatched it up with a frown. He jerked a glance at Lucky.

She met his stare for a heartbeat, then returned to her paperwork. Her job right now, like any good cop's, was to finish this report. She hooked her damp hair behind her ears and picked up her pen.

Besides, the last time she mentioned her dissatisfaction with the status quo, the sergeant had seized the opportunity to scare her with the bloodhound handler's nemesis, the dreaded budget cut. Despite the dramatically useful and irreplaceable work they did, bloodhounds were always seen as expendable when it came time to trim the operating budget. And this particular sergeant begrudged the dogs even the present modest allowance.

Flashier German shepherds were the vogue for tracking now, mostly because they were seen as more versatile. Bloodhounds did one thing only, trailing humans, and they did it well, but German shepherds could also be trained to smell out drugs and other contraband. Though the price for this versatility was diminished performance in both areas, the shepherds were seen as more cost effective and better public relations. Most departments with canine units already had them or were planning to get on the shepherd bandwagon.

She and her bloodhounds were continually on trial, and only their almost-routine heroics kept the man-trailing program alive. So far, by constant vigilance and vocal defense, she had managed to ward off any suggestion of cheapening the dogs' care and the purchase of inferior, less-expensive replacements. Though she needed to start training another puppy for the eventual retirement of aging Moonshine, she had insisted on a quality dog. But hadn't received one.

Perhaps that was all the more reason to argue for the chance to garner favorable publicity for the bloodhound program with a dramatic criminal case. If Cosmo or Moonshine could bring a rapist, murderer, or even a thief to justice instead of merely saving lives, public opinion might ensure their niche in the new budget.

But a glance over her shoulder at the sergeant convinced her that now was not the time to re-mount her soapbox. As his frown deepened to a scowl, he looked directly at her and flung the phone away from him as though it stank. "McCall!" His gravelly voice filled the room.

In spite of herself, Lucky started. She steeled herself to appear poised as she pushed back her chair and turned to face him. "Sir?"

He jerked his head to motion her forward. "Special assignment," he said.

Lucky's heart leaped. Whatever it was, the sergeant was clearly unhappy about it, which could mean a break for her. She rose, shifted the revolver at her side, and tried not to hurry to his desk.

But her shaky knees nearly betrayed her. She had not realized the depth of her weariness until she had rested for a few minutes. Now she wondered if her rubbery legs could manage to save her from disgrace. She forced her eyes to meet the sergeant's.

"What's the matter, McCall?" he snapped. "Job getting to be too much for you?" His steely eyes swept her muddy uniform pants and dirty fingernails. They lingered on the long hair he had repeatedly warned her to cut.

Lucky took a deep breath and said, "No, sir. I run two miles in the snow every day. And almost getting smashed by a freight train is all in a day's work for us *female* cops." *And I defy any man to easily shrug off an experience like that,* she finished to herself. But her indignation could not be swallowed, and she continued, "Sergeant, I am perfectly capable of any assignment you would give a male officer. I've had the same training and—"

"Save it, McCall." He held up his hand. "Your righteous indignation has been duly noted, but right now we have more important things to discuss." He jerked his head to the phone. "That was the boss. He wants you to take a dog to Arkansas. Seems a little *girl. . . .*"

Lucky noticed the unnecessary emphasis on the word, but struggled to keep her face emotionless. It was like him to bait her to a retort.

"She's got herself lost down there in the Ozark National Forest, and they seem to think they need a bloodhound to find her." He jabbed a stubby finger. "You're elected."

Lucky suppressed a gasp. "Thank you, sir."

He shook his head. "Don't thank me. The Arkansas State Police asked for bloodhound help from all the nearest metropolitan departments who have canine units." He met her eyes. "And you're it. You're all we can spare."

Thanks a lot, Lucky swallowed. And no doubt they figured that this little cakewalk would teach her a lesson. When she got back from the woods, they reasoned, she'd be sufficiently chastised to keep her mouth shut.

"You'll leave immediately," the sergeant added. "The Highway Patrol has a chopper on the way to pick you up." He turned back to the papers on his desk.

Lucky cleared her throat. "Sergeant, I need both dogs."

He looked up, his face stony.

Before he could speak, Lucky rushed on: "Especially for a job like this, in heavy country, I can't ask one dog to work without a backup. And that far away, I can't depend on one dog not being injured or—"

"One dog, McCall. This little caper will play havoc with my budget as it is. Dismissed." His glance shifted to the papers in front of him.

Lucky took a deep breath and bit her lip. She worked to keep her voice low and even. "You're almost guaranteeing failure, Sergeant." She knew the sergeant was considering more than his budget. He wanted her to fail. He thought she had no chance of finding the little girl, anyway, and a bloodhound failure now would give him the ammunition he needed to replace her and her dogs. *German shepherds, here we come.*

"Dismissed, Officer McCall," he said without looking up.

Chapter Two

*A*t the first mention of Arkansas, Lucky had slammed a door in her mind. She had worked too hard to forget him, and had too much to do too quickly to waste time remembering King. She had come too far from him to backtrack now.

But while she checked harnesses and assembled leads, paw dressings, and other gear, she struggled against the memories. Choosing which dog should go required a judgment unclouded by the kind of teary softness that sometimes accompanied thoughts of Kingston Wynn. Arkansas was a big place, and the chances of running into King were small.

Who do you think you're kidding? she asked herself. *You know you heard he was assigned to the Ozark National Forest.* She pushed away the thought and went out to the dog pen, studying the sky as she stepped into the darkness. The snow had stopped, but the clouds lingered. That was good, for perhaps it would not be too cold. The child might have a chance.

Lucky flipped on the outside lights and squatted to study the two bloodhounds vying for her attention. The Ozark National Forest was a big place divided into several units. All were heavily forested, hilly terrain, rough country. The chances of a successful trail under those conditions were slight.

Cosmo pushed between her and Moonshine and studied her face thoughtfully. His drooping bloodhound eyes always seemed to look into her and know her thoughts. No German shepherd could be as affectionate or as loyal and hardworking. She fondled his long silky ear and wondered if his youth would make up for the lack of rest after tonight's trail. One by one she picked up his big paws and inspected them for cuts and sores.

By rights, big red Moonshine should go. She had the depth of experience, gained from hundreds of difficult trails. Lucky scratched under Moonshine's loose-skinned chin and was rewarded with a grin. "You're the old pro, aren't you, girl?" The dog leaned against her leg and sighed. The wrinkly skin on Moonshine's forehead sagged in a look of concern. *After all we've been through together,* the older hound's attitude seemed to say, *you can't possibly even consider taking that upstart.*

King would choose Moonshine, Lucky thought, and hated it. *Forget about him,* she told herself savagely. She had managed that for some time. Why did she have to be distracted now, when she had critical decisions to make and important things to do?

Though all he knew about bloodhounds was what she had told him, King would go with experience and steadiness and dependability. Lucky shook her head as if to clear it and jumped up. Cosmo had proved himself ready. And the way he'd obeyed her commands today showed that he could be trusted. He was young and strong and would run the trail until he dropped. A child's life might depend on that. It would be cruel to take Moonshine on such a potentially grueling search. She had earned the easy ones.

Cosmo's big forepaw stepped on her foot possessively and he wedged Moonshine away. "Okay, boy." Lucky slapped Cosmo's beefy rump. "You're elected. You're going to Arkansas."

Arkansas. National Forest. Forest ranger. King. Sometimes it was hard to remember why she had chosen this life over him. The life of a woman cop, unappreciated and harassed.

Stop this! she ordered herself, and strode angrily out of the dog pen. She banged the gate into place and snapped the lock firmly, intending it also to exclude the troublesome thoughts of King.

She had no time to waste in daydreaming of what might have been. The chopper was on its way and she must be ready. A child's life depended on her and her dogs and on the important job she believed in and had chosen above all else.

As she packed the equipment and clothing from her locker, a new worry intruded. Just as Cosmo would represent the bloodhound breed on this case, she, too, would be on trial. The other searchers would no doubt be dismayed to see a woman get off that chopper in Arkansas. How she handled herself, her dog, and this search might well affect her career and her whole life.

She caught herself up short. Memories of King must be bringing these long-conquered self-doubts to the surface again. *All the more reason to put him out of your mind once and for all,* she told herself firmly. Wasn't she a highly trained, experienced, and competent law-enforcement officer? Wasn't she a knowledgeable, well-regarded bloodhound handler, respected and confident?

You're not a greenhorn rookie anymore, she assured herself. *You're a pro. You know what you're doing. You'll go down there and show those people— those men—how it should be done. Cosmo's one of the best and you trained him. You both can handle it.*

Like an Achilles' heel, King had been her weak spot from the day she met him. Why couldn't this search have been someplace safe like Siberia, or anywhere but Arkansas?

She thought again of the little girl alone in the

dark forest, and her heart lurched. The child would be frightened, and cold, and close to death.

Lucky slammed the locker door. The longer the trail aged, the slimmer the child's chances became. Where was that helicopter? Why hadn't they called in a local search-and-rescue team and gotten a hound in those woods right away? She would be on the trail at daybreak, but if she couldn't sleep in the chopper, she'd be dead on her feet and no good to the little girl or anyone else. Cosmo deserved a competent handler, and so did the lost child.

When the highway-patrol helicopter touched down, she and Cosmo were ready and waiting. Once the bloodhound was introduced to the two highway-patrol officers and allowed to sniff them, he tolerated their lifting him into the chopper. Lucky explained that the dog catalogued and remembered individual scents as humans do names and faces. If he ever saw or smelled them again, he would recognize them.

Grateful that they occupied the front seat and each other so that she wouldn't be required to make small talk, Lucky settled herself and Cosmo in the rear on a small jump seat not designed for long-legged cops and long-eared monster dogs. Dimly lit, the interior of the helicopter seemed a purgatory of sound. She probably wouldn't sleep but she was determined to rest and use the flight time to Arkansas to plan her approach to this case. She wished for more details of the child's disappearance, for she must leave no room for doubt of her competence. She must be assertive, firm, and display a take-charge attitude. She must meet the other searchers confidently, handle Cosmo authoritatively. And above all, they must find the child.

Once away from the city lights, the helicopter climbed and increased its speed. Conversation would be impossible over the roar of the craft except by radio. Earphones hung near her head and danced crazily in the thrumming power of the engine. Finding a blanket wadded into a corner, she huddled against a chill draft. Opting for a down vest on the flight instead of her uniform coat had been an error of judgment, unlike her usual practicality.

There would probably be a meeting to touch base with the other searchers and organize their attack. She could handle that, because she was accustomed to endless meetings and to the necessity for explaining how the hounds worked and what kind of support she must have.

Unsettled by the noise and vibrations under and around him and by this departure from routine, Cosmo crowded beside her on the seat. He forced his heavy, wet nose under her arm and wriggled into a hug and a share of the blanket. The loose skin on his head slumped into wrinkles and gave him a distinctly worried look. Lucky fondled a silky black ear and murmured reassurance. She had long ago ceased to be concerned about dog hair and slobbers on her uniform.

But what if she did, indeed, run into King? Every mile took her closer to that possibility even though she hadn't seen or heard from him since that last camping trip, taken in this same Ozark National Forest. She had loved him so much then, but she was so sure that she could forget him and find somebody else, somebody who wouldn't ask her to give up her chosen way of life.

But she hadn't. And, as she had been so painfully reminded, neither had she forgotten him. Like a dike breached by a tiny fault, her mind let the memories come flooding in the moment she let down her guard.

From the moment they met, on their first day of college at the University of Arkansas, she and Kingston Wynn had known that they were soul mates. They came from similar backgrounds, though his family had stayed in Arkansas and hers had moved to Missouri when her father decided to become a cop. She had decided to attend college in her home state to renew her ties there—and because she was homesick, she could now admit.

She and King had been inseparable from the beginning. Because their course work paralleled to some extent—hers in criminal law and his in forestry and law enforcement—they shared some classes, and every waking minute. She had loved

King's sense of humor, his gentleness, the way he was so much a man and yet, in many ways, almost boyish.

Every girl in school had hated her because King was the most dashing and handsome guy and he was hers. It wasn't that he was movie-star handsome, necessarily, but he was certainly good-looking in a rugged, outdoorsy way—dark curly hair, green eyes that seemed to look right into her, a nice physique.

And more than her boyfriend, King had been her *friend,* the best friend she had ever had. Ironically, it was King's rescue of a scrawny bloodhound puppy from a shelter that first awakened her love for the breed and its capabilities.

He, on his part, had been delighted with her love of the outdoors, her understanding and affection for animals, and her sharing of his total dedication to the conservation ethic. Later, Lucky was to wonder why King hadn't questioned her constant remarks about becoming a police officer. Women were still not accepted in small-town police work, especially in King's Ozarks, and she later learned that sometimes they were barely tolerated in the city. Surely he knew that she would not be content to become a dispatcher in the local sheriff's office.

Ever since she was a little girl she had dreamed of following in her father's footsteps. Because Dad had no sons, he had raised her to be a cop like him and his father before him. After Dad was injured in the line of duty and confined to a wheelchair, the department began to pay for her education. As a result, she felt obligated to them, and she certainly couldn't let Dad down.

And when she had discovered and fallen in love with man-trailing bloodhounds during college, and then learned that she could combine them with law enforcement, she had sacrificed King. She would never forget his face when she told him of her decision.

It was spring break of their senior year and they had gone canoe camping in the national forest. There had been many other camping trips, but this was to be their last as college students, and King wanted it to be special, something to remember, something to talk about on their fiftieth anniversary.

The dawn was still gray, with the mists shifting above the river as they stowed their camping gear and launched the canoe. Sitting in the front, huddled against the river chill in a down jacket over her life vest, Lucky had paddled and watched for hazards in the water. As he paddled from the rear of the canoe, King could steer and control their progress over or around white-water rapids or other obstructions.

For a while they had not spoken. The beauty and fragility of the dawn needed no discussion, and the silence of nature became their own. Only the muffled sounds of their paddles dipping in and out of the river disturbed the perfect peace. Beside them towered the great stone bluff, its top disappearing into the mist and reminding Lucky of the river's power.

She spotted a muskrat returning to its den, and she turned to see if King had noticed. He nodded and smiled. The opposite bank slid by, forested but still winter-bare. Here and there the green of cedars and pines punctuated the leafless trees. A doe heavy with her fawn watched curiously as they floated silently past. Overhead, an eagle launched from its rocky perch near the top of the bluff and sailed between them and the rising sun. Its triumphant, solitary cry sounded like "free!" Lucky thought that canoeing, quiet and nonintrusive, like tiptoeing into a painting, must be the perfect way to get close to nature.

Gradually the pink-rouged mists rose to meet the sun, and Lucky shed her jacket. With the coming of full daylight they spoke softly of the spectacular river scenery and the glimpses allowed them by nature. When the sun became warm on their faces, they beached the canoe easily on a wide, smooth sandbar and unloaded their breakfast supplies. Lucky breathed deeply of the earthy aroma of warm river gravel.

"Look." King touched her shoulder and pointed. A dogwood tree in full bloom leaned over the water a little way downstream. His green eyes danced with pleasure.

Lucky caught her breath at its beauty. The wilderness pressed around them, another blossoming dogwood almost shockingly white against the green of a giant cedar. "There's another one," she said. "Our timing is perfect this year. This has got to be the most beautiful spot in all creation."

King nodded and grinned. "At least this morning it is." His fingers brushed her cheek. "And you've the most beautiful face in all creation." His voice was soft with emotion.

Lucky smiled into his eyes. "Aw, shucks." She turned her head to kiss his callused hand. "Where's my cook wood?"

He sighed. "All right, my little Indian princess, I'll get it."

She snorted. "Indian princess! I doubt if you've seen many blue-eyed Indians." She tilted her head to study his inky hair and the skin perpetually tanned by his outdoor life. "Except for all those curls, you qualify on that score better than I."

He shook his head. "Blue eyes or not, this morning, with your hair hanging down and those high cheekbones, you put me in mind of a lovely Indian maiden." He pulled her to him in a hug. "I almost wish you were. Then we could stay here in the wilderness and never have to go back."

Lucky caught the note of sadness in his voice and hugged him back. His face was thoughtful. The laugh lines around his mouth seemed deeper, and for the first time she noticed tiny crow's feet when he squinted in the dazzling sunlight.

She rubbed her chin against the rough flannel of his shirt. "Hey, come on, let's cook. I'm starved." She pushed away. "If you'll get a fire going, I'll find the skillet and the bacon."

After breakfast he patted his stomach and grinned at her. "You really are something. I'm the one they should call lucky."

He stepped behind her and put a hand on each of her shoulders. He turned her to face the bluff across the river and pointed. "Sight along my arm," he said. "See where that old den tree leans a little over the edge of the bluff? There's a dogwood a little to one side and a big sycamore."

"I see it," Lucky replied, hooking a hand over his muscular arm. "What am I looking at?"

He pulled her back against him and wrapped his arms around her. "Your future castle, princess," he said softly against her ear. "The future home of Mr. and Mrs. Kingston Wynn." His voice had become husky. "There's a pocket of land up there that's been in my family for years. I'm going to build us a castle of native stone and cedar, and it's gonna have—"

"King, wait." She tried to turn in his arms.

"I know—we can't afford it. Well, maybe we can't—yet. But someday we'll build up there, and all of this"—he swept an arm around them—"will be our front yard. In the meantime we'll camp up there every chance we get."

Lucky broke his grasp and turned to face him. "King, I thought you understood. I've never made any secret of it." His expression almost stopped her, but she knew there would never be an easier time. "I'm going back to Kansas City. Dad's counting on me. The police department is expecting me, and I'm obligated to join up."

"But you love it here just as much as I do." His voice was very low and his eyes were terrible, like a dog's when it has been hit by a car.

She nodded and bit her lip to keep from sobbing. "Of course. And I love you."

His breath rushed out as though she had punched him in the stomach. "Then why . . . ?"

"Surely you've known from the beginning. You've always known. I've always said I was going back to Kansas City and. . . ." She reached out a trembling hand.

He jerked out of her reach and turned away. At his sides his fists clenched and unclenched. He lifted his face to the sky and took a deep breath. The only sound was the murmur of the river's current rushing around their rocky outcropping.

Lucky went to him. "King. . . ."

"I need to be alone for a while," he said. "You'll be all right here. I'll be back." He strode away without looking at her, the forest swallowing him from view remarkably soon.

She blinked back tears. For almost four years she had known this day would come. She had thought herself prepared for it. Now she wondered if she would ever recover from it. But giving up the dreams of a lifetime and betraying her invalid father seemed equally impossible. Maybe she'd been brainwashed. Maybe she'd read too much feminist literature. She knew only that she must live her own life, find her own dream.

She had tossed her head with a sigh and steeled herself to have the courage of her convictions. She paced the narrow rock ledge until the pain subsided slightly, and then realized she felt cold. And utterly lonely. By the time she unloaded the camping gear and built a small fire, shadows had gathered below the bluff. Mist began to form over the river. She pitched their twin tents as far from the water's edge as she could manage.

Then she huddled over the fire, watching shadows dance in the woods and yearning for King. Once she glanced to the top of the forbidding bluff and saw him standing on the site of his dream house. *God, help him,* she prayed. *I hope he finds someone who'll appreciate his dream house with him.*

Finally he returned, calling cheerfully for supper and full of plans for the next day. Lucky struggled to match his mood. He was right. There was no need to waste the time they had left to be together.

After supper they sat on a log before the fire for

a long time. The strain of making conversation began to tell, and the silence deepened with the darkness. The fire burned low. The White River slapped gently against the shore and made soft sucking sounds under a rocky ledge.

King stretched and squatted beside the firepit. He stirred the embers, and by the reflected light Lucky saw the pain shining in his eyes. He turned and sat back on his heels beside her. "I don't think I can live without you, Lucky."

She reached to smooth back the shock of dark curls that had fallen over his forehead. "This is the modern world, the real world, and not a fairy tale. I have to lead my own life and it's not here."

"But I can't leave here." His voice sounded strangled.

She shook her head. "No, of course you can't. I never really dared hope you could." Even as she said it, she had wondered if it were true.

That was five years ago. By unspoken agreement, because they had sensed that it would only prove painful to keep in touch, there had been no contact since. Mutual friends had kept her informed of his whereabouts and that he was still unmarried. Several had made it a point to tell her when he was promoted to head ranger on the Sylamore unit of the Ozark National Forest. He had what he wanted.

Did *she?* There were times, like earlier in the sergeant's office, when she wondered if she had been wrong to sacrifice such a man for such an imperfect realization of her goals and dreams. Ever since King, the other men in her life had failed to measure up. All had been either too weak or too demanding, or too selfish or too chauvinistic. There had never been a man who could love her and still let her be her own person and an equal partner.

If they were to meet again, would he hate her enough to let the past stand in the way of her finding this poor lost little girl?

Chapter Three

A scent article! Lucky jerked awake in the helicopter as though someone had snapped his fingers in front of her nose. She should have thought of it much sooner. These people might have no experience working with bloodhounds. While the trail aged, she had no wish to lose valuable time in driving for miles after a scent article when they should be running the trail.

Throwing off the blanket, she sat up straight. Cosmo grunted his displeasure at being disturbed. She jerked the headphone off its hook and clapped it on her head. Fumbling with the mike button, she cursed herself for allowing memories of Kingston Wynn to interfere with her performance as a police officer. If she hadn't been so preoccupied with thoughts of him, she would have been more alert. A child's life might depend on her and the help she could give the amazing nose beside her.

She pressed the microphone button. "Excuse me, Captain," she said to interrupt the conversation of the two men. "I need to radio ahead some important instructions." She released the button and returned the gaze of the officer in the right seat, who had turned to stare at her. His lips moved.

"We're almost there," she heard in her earphones. "Maybe another thirty minutes." Cosmo extended his massive nose and sniffed the plastic that managed to speak.

Lucky pressed her button and said, "Long enough to be important." She saw no reason to explain to these men that if she hadn't been so lost in foolish memories, it would have been hours ago. Anger and frustration with her lapse stiffened her voice and helped convince the highway patrol to put in the call.

As she listened to the exchange of radio signals with the ground ahead of them, she took a deep breath. No more daydreaming. No more King. She couldn't let his presence, real or imagined, ruin her performance on this case. A child's life was on the line. She must be as hard as nails. Even if she ran into King, there must be no emotion, no more interference with the job she had to do.

"This is Sheriff Wayne Posey," said a voice in her ears, a deep, smooth voice with soft, Southern overtones. "Go ahead. We're ready for your instructions. Over."

Lucky cleared her throat before pushing the mike button. "Sheriff, this is Officer McCall, the bloodhound handler. My dog will need a scent article, something bearing the scent of the person he's to find. Is the subject's family available there? Over."

"No, the family was over at the Blanchard Springs campground in the national forest, but they went to stay with friends last night. Over."

Lucky groaned. The only way to be certain Cosmo had an article holding only the scent of the human for whom he searched, uncontaminated by other confusing scents, was to collect it herself. But in this case that would consume time she didn't have. Already the child must be cold and endangered.

The earphones crackled again. "To be real honest with you, Officer McCall, we're not familiar with working with dogs. Tell me what you need, and I'll have it when you touch down. Over." The voice sounded professional, determined.

"Sheriff, ask the child's family for an article of her clothing to give the hound her scent, something she wore for a while, preferably next to her body. Something that hasn't been washed, but tell them not—repeat, *not*—to get it out of the laundry where it would be mixed up with the scent of others. Choose something that only the child has handled if at all possible. Her nightgown would do. Tell them to pick it up with a fork or pliers, tie it inside a plastic bag, and bring it to search headquarters. Immediately. Our estimated time of arrival is less than thirty minutes. Any questions? Over." She looked out the window as if she could watch the sheriff's response, but saw only her own reflection in the glass. A gray crack had opened in the blackness along the eastern horizon.

"Roger. No questions, Officer McCall. Read you five by five. I've got the address. I'll send a man out there immediately. Over." The sheriff sounded grim, as though he realized that he should have been more aware of the need for an article on which to scent the bloodhound.

Remarkable as he was, Cosmo had to know for whom he was searching. Lucky wished she had asked Sheriff Posey to keep everyone away from the area where the trail might begin. There were many things she had done wrong already. She hoped she could make up for the time she had lost mooning over King.

As if sensing her distress, Cosmo cuddled closer. His wrinkled brow and droopy jowls gave him an air of perpetual sadness. He whimpered softly and licked her hand. She hugged him and scratched a floppy ear. "Won't be long now, boy," she whispered. "But these woods are different from our city variety."

She looked down at the sea of trees now visible below them. Like monstrous ocean waves, the hills undulated for as far as she could see in any direction. They were even more beautiful than she remembered. *The hills of home,* she thought. She hadn't known how much she missed them. And King.

Lucky's ears popped as the helicopter descended. She watched Cosmo for signs of discomfort, but saw none. The breed was so adaptable, such a bundle of fine and remarkable traits. If a bloodhound really was as sad as he looked, it was probably because he had been the victim of such bad press over the years. Even when a hero, he was often depicted as a bloodthirsty beast, because that made for more dramatic copy than did his true nature, that of a gentle giant. How many more lives might be saved if people only knew how really amazing he was.

Lucky waited until the rotors had stopped before she dismounted with Cosmo; he would be assailed with enough strange smells, sounds, and sights without coping with the blade wash. But the hound lifted his nose and moved forward to greet the strangers crowding around them.

One man towered above the rest. A big, white Stetson emphasized his height and the width of his shoulders. A highly polished badge gleamed in the weak light of the new dawn. Cosmo lifted his nose and inhaled deeply. To Lucky's astonishment, the dog growled softly deep in his throat. Though it was customary for him to reserve judgment before making up with a new person, she had never known him to greet a stranger with hostility. Bloodhounds loved everyone; they were not natural guard dogs.

Lucky extended her hand. "Sheriff Posey? I'm Officer McCall, but call me Lucky." She pointed to the dog at her thigh. "This is Cosmo. We want to get right to work. We've lost too much time already." She hoped her voice sounded firm and professional, in control but not bossy.

The sheriff touched the brim of his hat. A few years ago he would have smiled condescendingly, murmured a "ma'am," and spoken to the men beside her. Now he looked her in the eye. "Officer McCall—Lucky, we're ready here." He jerked his head to a group of men standing some distance apart from the helicopter. "I've assembled our search team out here in order to save transport time. I thought you'd want to hit the ground running, so to speak."

Lucky nodded. "Good thinking, Sheriff. That I do. Cosmo has lost too much time already." She reached into the chopper and hefted her pack, slipping the strap over her shoulder. Then she fell into step beside Posey as he paced away. Cosmo heeled as a matter of course, his leash slack between them. He watched the sheriff closely.

She glanced up, aware of the sheriff's polished, clean-cut good looks. *Like a great, blond bear,* she thought. "Just how old is this trail?" she asked him.

Without breaking stride he lifted his watch and turned his wrist to catch the light from the runway marker. "Just under twenty-four hours. Apparently she wandered out of the camper early yesterday morning, before anybody else woke up. Is that gonna be a problem?"

Lucky took a deep breath. "Maybe not. Cosmo has successfully run older trails, but not in this terrain. The scent could have blown all over by now, from the ridge tops to the valleys or vice versa. And a bloodhound trails the scent. He doesn't track footprints the way a German shepherd does. It sure would have been easier if we'd been on it sooner." She worked to keep the irritation from her voice. "Tell me something, Sheriff, why haven't you called in a volunteer search-and-rescue group, someone closer, with a bloodhound? Every second counts in a situation like this."

He halted abruptly and touched her arm to stop her.

Again Lucky was surprised to hear Cosmo give a low warning growl.

"Look," he said. "This is the hills, okay? We don't have a lot of population, and the ones we do have aren't running around playing cops and robbers, so to speak, like in some other places. And bloodhounds ain't too popular in these parts." He jerked his head to indicate they should keep walking. "When the kid was reported missing, we rounded up a bunch of people and started combing the area, thinking she couldn't have gotten too far. When I saw we were looking for a needle in a haystack, I remembered an article about bloodhounds that I had read in a police magazine." He lifted a big hand and dropped it. "Okay, so I should have called sooner, but I called."

Lucky bit her lip and shot a glance to the hills surrounding the small airfield and then to the purple clouds beginning to appear in a graying sky. It would take a half hour to move to the campground and get ready, and it would be daylight by then. She checked her watch. "What's the weather been like, yesterday and last night? What's the forecast?"

Posey groaned. "Yesterday was cool and wet, rained all day." He clucked his tongue. "I wouldn't have wanted to be out in it. Today, rain again. Lots of it. Fog. And cooler, maybe turning to snow. More rotten luck." He regarded her from under the brim of his hat as though wanting to ask what a woman was doing in a situation like this.

"On the contrary, Sheriff, although it is bad for the child. Bloodhounds trail better when it's damp and cool than when it's dry and hot. The scent behaves differently. He can handle the weather." She added silently, *But can I?*

When he made no reply, Lucky knew he was wondering the same thing.

Another thought struck her, another need she should have anticipated in Kansas City. "Sheriff, I'll need topographic maps of this whole area, and a map of the national forest."

He nodded. "I did think of that. I got 'em for you. They're over here at my squad car. And a radio. Anything else? We've been lookin' for that little girl all yesterday and all last night. In these hills and these woods. . . ." He came to a stop and his eyes sought hers. His were a curious light brown, almost an amber. "You and your hound are our only hope, Lucky." Something in his voice said that he'd already given up, whether at the sight of her or otherwise. "And I sure hope you are. Lucky, I mean."

As they approached the group at the edge of the tarmac, she was aware that they were all men. Despite her resolve to put King out of her mind, she found herself searching for his face in the crowd.

When she halted, Cosmo gathered his huge haunches under him and sat erect at her left knee as she had trained him. His nose worked at sorting out the scents of those assembled around them. Occasionally he rolled his eyes toward Posey.

The sheriff turned to Lucky. "Fellas, this is Officer McCall from the Kansas City police. I won't waste time with individual introductions. She's gonna tell us what we need to know to work with this here dog." He inclined his head to Lucky and stepped back a few paces. As an afterthought he stepped forward again. "And I just want say, this little lady . . . er, this officer and her dog, they tell me—that is, her supervisor tells me—have found a heap of missing folks." He stepped back.

Lucky nodded to the men, aware that all eyes were on her and Cosmo. "Call me Lucky," she said. She shivered, and hoped it was from the chill wind beginning to whip dust devils across the runway, a wind that might complicate things even more for Cosmo. Moonshine might have handled it better.

She chased away the thought; the last thing she needed was to lose confidence in her dog, the dog she had chosen and trained, the one she herself had selected to do this job. But if the wind shifted to the south, perhaps no bloodhound could follow the trail.

She cleared her throat and swung her pack to the pavement. "There's not much to tell you. The dog does the work. I just hang on, watch for trouble, and radio back when we find her." She tried to focus on an individual face in the dim light. "You can help by staying out of the search area to avoid confusing the scent. The less car exhaust, gasoline fumes, cigarette smoke, and the like that he has to contend with, the better. And I need backup, at least one person to run with me and the dog in case of trouble or injury. Someone to be my eyes and ears while my full attention is on the hound. Someone to man the radio, relay messages, or ask for help if I've got my hands full. Someone armed." She searched their faces. "Someone in good physical condition who can run for miles, maybe, in those woods." She jerked her head to the hill behind her, its peak hidden in the morning mist so common in the Ozarks.

Fully aware that country people did not like to hear of "how we do it in the city," she decided not to add that ideally there should be a backup *team* to keep in constant touch with headquarters by radio, to man the maps and compass, and to keep track of her whereabouts at all times.

The men shifted their feet and exchanged glances. One of them asked, "How come you can't just turn 'im loose and let 'im run like a coonhound, and then go in when he makes the find?"

Lucky took a deep breath. "In the first place, the bloodhound has no road sense. He single-mindedly follows the trail he has been assigned, with no thought for his own safety. He'll run into traffic, trees, barbed-wire fencing, a river too deep or too cold to swim if that's where the trail leads. And this loose skin on his head"—she lifted a fold of Cosmo's brow—"falls forward when his head is down. It and his big, floppy ears are designed to form a sort of cup to capture and hold the scent. But that means he can scarcely see."

She looked around the group. "His handler— me, in this case—is his eyes and ears and better judgment. *He's* the nose. I've been told that his nose may be two or three million times better than ours. Bloodhounds can follow one person's scent through a crowded airport or a football stadium. They've been bred and trained for centuries to do just one thing—trail humans. And what they can do with that nose is nothing short of amazing."

She glanced around the group, but no one met her gaze. She continued: "And in the second place, bloodhounds work silently. They don't bay on the trail or bark when they've found their quarry. No matter what you've seen in the movies or on TV, kid or criminal, when he's found he's more likely to get a big kiss."

The eastern sky blushed pink, but the sun did not show its face. "Time's awastin'," Lucky finished. "Who's going to run with us to find this little girl?" Again she sought eye contact with a few of the men.

No one spoke.

Lucky shouldered her pack. "Well, Sheriff, looks like you're elected by default." She glanced up at him. "Let's go."

The sheriff blinked and shifted on his feet. "Me? Why, I gotta lead the other searchers, so to speak, and. . . ."

A man behind him guffawed. "Come on, Sheriff! Here's your chance to be a hero and get reelected."

"Yeah, Tank, and here's where you can prove what great shape you're in, just like you're always tellin' us," another chimed in. "Deputy Marks knows the game plan."

Posey lifted his Stetson and resettled it firmly. "Okay, little . . . Lucky, lead on."

The men laughed and cheered. Cosmo lifted his nose and bayed at the uproar. Lucky touched his head. "Cosmo, heel." She turned her back on the group of men and pivoted to the sheriff. "Sheriff, we're wasting time here. I need transport to the place where the child was last seen."

At the campground inside the national forest, Lucky refused to consider that she was now on King's home turf. She left Cosmo in the sheriff's cruiser to inspect the scene. "Where's the ranger in charge of this area?" she asked Posey.

"He radioed a while ago to find out your time of arrival. Said he'd meet us here." He peered up the mist-shrouded road.

Lucky groaned. The ground around the family's camper and for as far as she could see in any direction had been trampled by the feet of dozens of searchers. The cars, Jeeps, and pickups of seemingly a dozen law-enforcement agencies had crossed and crisscrossed the entire area for twenty-four hours and now lined the narrow winding drive leading into the depths of the campground.

She glanced at the sky. Full daylight had been delayed by a bank of heavy clouds piling up in the north. The barometer was probably dropping. The wind had quieted, but still swirled the mist rising in the valley. So far it was still out of the north.

She shook her head. "Sheriff, I hate to tell you that things don't look too good. This whole setup"—she waved an arm to include the entire heavily trafficked area—"is like a bad dream. It's a textbook case of how not to start a bloodhound."

The sheriff reset his Stetson. "So what are you saying? You're gonna quit before you even get started?" His voice was sharp.

She gave him a look that she hoped was sufficiently withering. "Of course not." She didn't bother to mask the irritation in her voice. "I'm advising you, as one professional to another, that our chances of trailing this child are less than ideal."

"Is there anything we can do?"

Lucky took a deep breath and studied the sandy ground, which might be moist enough to hold a footprint. "Where was the child last seen? Where did you start searching yesterday? How did you know what direction to take?"

He jerked his head to the wide, riverlike stream flowing past the campground. "Nobody saw her head for it, but the logical place to start was Sylamore Creek, which her parents said had fascinated her." He circled a hand over his head. "We combed both banks all up and down here. There was a small footprint that we took to be hers, mainly because we didn't have anything else to go on, and we started off in that direction."

She watched him through narrowed eyes. "I suppose you considered the possibility. . . ."

"Yeah, sure, but the water here is as clear as glass. You can see the bottom anywhere, no matter how deep it is. I had a hundred men on that creek all day. The ranger got hold of a chopper and they flew up and down the creek, but didn't see anything. 'Course, they couldn't see a thing in the trees. Not a sign of her."

"Show me the footprint," Lucky said, even though it had probably been obliterated by the searchers. "Of course, it could belong to anyone, not just the missing girl."

To her surprise, the sheriff had roped off a few square feet around the tiny footprint, the mark of a sneaker or tennis shoe, in the moist rocky beach of the creek. She studied the tread of the footprint in order to recognize another like it later on. But why were there no other prints? The ground around the solitary print was equally soft and should bear the imprint of the next step. She peered into the water and searched for similar markings in the streambed.

"The current's pretty fast along here," Tank pointed out. "Besides, the print is parallel to the water."

"Just how old is this child, Tank?" Lucky asked as she knelt to inspect the indentation in the cherty soil.

He squatted beside her. "The mother says she's almost three, and that she's fascinated by the water and the woods, and she likes the squirrels and lizards. That's why we thought. . . ." He jerked his head to the woods.

She nodded. "It's worth a try. No point wasting time back there." She flicked a glance to the camping area.

Gazing around her, Lucky studied the terrain. They were in a wide bend of the creek, a rocky flat bounded by the steep bluff of the stream and by deep woods that pressed down to the very edges of the campsites on its shore. But the footprint pointed to a sliver of open area along the creek. Almost a gravel bar, it gradually narrowed as the creek flowed into a boulder-choked hollow. How could such a small child get so far so fast without being seen? And all around them the hills rose precipitously, dark and forbidding under the lowering sky. Surely not very enticing to a three-year-old.

Tank straightened. "What do you need?"

She got to her feet and looked up at him. "I need that scent article. And keep everyone away from this area. If there's any way you can manage it, try to keep hikers or bystanders out of the woods until the search is over."

Behind her, King's velvet voice said, "I can manage it."

Although she thought herself prepared for this encounter, a forbidden thrill stabbed through her. She turned slowly to prepare herself for the shock of seeing him, and she tried to look somewhere near his face instead of into his eyes. "Hello, King," she said.

He touched the brim of his camouflage bill cap. "Hello, Officer McCall. Welcome to Ozark National Forest." His voice seemed tightly controlled.

"What else can I do for you? Do you need a backup? I know those hills like—"

"I'm gonna back her up," Tank said, and squared his shoulders. His eyes narrowed, and his face betrayed that his mind was busy analyzing the fact that they knew each other.

King lifted an eyebrow. "That so?" He inclined his head to the sheriff's feet. "Then I suggest that you find something to wear other than cowboy boots." His gaze flickered back to Lucky's face. "Any trouble with the locals?"

"No, but I think they're all privately laughing up their sleeves." By looking at the brim of his cap, she could avoid the depths of his hypnotic emerald eyes. "But I'm used to that."

King lifted his chin and scanned the sky. "It doesn't look good for that kid, Lucky."

She shook her head. "But we can't just write her off. I'm going in." She knew he had forgotten Tank's presence. It was as though the last five years had never been.

"I figured you would." King took a step nearer, then stopped. He seemed to be searching for words.

She fought the urge to step back, remembering her determination not to let the past intrude on the vital work to be done here. "I want to get started immediately."

"Okay. I'll coordinate things here and stand by the radio in case you need me. Have you got the frequencies and everything you need?" His soft voice had hardened to the businesslike tone he probably used for everyone.

Tank cleared his throat. "I'm taking care of her, Wynn." He sought Lucky's gaze. "I got some running shoes in the car. It won't take me long to change." His eyes narrowed. "You sure you're really in condition to take this one on?"

Before Lucky could reply, King said, "You better believe she is, Posey. You'll be doing good to keep up with her." His glance slid from Tank to Lucky's face. "She knows what she's doing."

Lucky looked into King's eyes. A shock went through her, but she maintained control. "Could you locate another hound?" she asked. "If anything goes wrong up there"—she tilted her head to the misty mountains across the creek—"and my dog gets out of commission, then that poor kid won't have much of a chance to survive."

King inspected his boots. "I can't find any that aren't busy somewhere else, Lucky. The search-and-rescue group at Sedalia went to Menninger's to help find a wandering patient, and the bunch from Miller Falls went to Colorado yesterday to look for some lost hikers. That's why I called your department. I don't know of any others. Do you?" His eyes searched her face.

She shook her head and made a mental note to consider later why the handsome sheriff had lied to her. "Only the team in St. Louis, but they went to help Louisville find flood victims. And their police department converted to German shepherds." She swallowed the rest, that shepherds would be almost worthless in this situation.

As King pushed back his cap, a dark curl escaped under the brim. "Anybody else would be too far away to do any good. By the time they got here. . . ." He shook his head.

Lucky took a deep breath. "Looks like Cosmo and I are elected for this one. All the way."

Chapter Four

*K*ing took another step closer. "Will I see you later, after this is over?" His voice was lower, softer, the way it used to be when he held her in his arms.

Lucky closed her eyes a moment to block the sight of his face and the lock of hair she wanted to brush from his brow. She recalled her intention to concentrate solely on the lost child. "King, I—"

A siren echoed in the hollow and bounced between the hills. It seemed to fill the tiny valley and her head. *This will be the scent article,* she thought, and pushed away the awareness of King. She remembered the sheriff and glanced up at his square jaw. "Let's go," she told him, and with Tank at her heels, she crunched across the gravel bar to his cruiser. She half turned to see King heading for his government-green pickup truck, then strengthened her resolve to think only of the job at hand.

The deputy's big white car filled the campground road, and after swaying around a last tight curve, it stopped only feet from them. As its wide door swung open, Lucky sidestepped the flash of gold-painted emblem bearing the sheriff's seal. A deputy emerged with a bulging bread bag.

"Is that the scent article?" Lucky asked.

The deputy nodded. "But the family says the little girl was wearing her nightgown. Everything else was in the laundry bag except these—her socks and underpants."

"Perfect." She pivoted to the sheriff's car and retrieved her pack. Cosmo greeted her return with a long bay. He pranced along the backseat and pressed his nose against the window glass. She saw that his slobbers had marked all the windows as he had followed her progress around the site. He knew there was a trail to be run, and rather than lie quietly as he would do at home, he pushed against the front seat eagerly. When Lucky pulled his special trailing harness from the pack, his heavy tail thumped against the side of the car.

But before she could harness him, a car came careening around the campground road, its horn blaring. It stopped inches behind the deputy's cruiser, and the woman behind the wheel leaped into the road without closing the door. "Sheriff!" she screeched. She tugged a sweater across her print dress and brushed back tendrils of uncombed hair. "Tank Posey, how could you do this?" she demanded. "How can you stand there and—"

"Whoa." Tank held up both hands as though to ward off the woman's attack. "What's all this?"

She flung an arm at Cosmo, who was watching her through the car window. "How could you send that vicious beast out after our little Amy?"

Lucky took a deep breath and stepped away from the cruiser. Up close, she saw that the woman's face was tear-stained, her eyes red. "Excuse me, ma'am," she said. "Are you the mother of the lost child?" She worked to keep her voice low and even.

The woman looked her up and down distastefully. "Her aunt. You take your bloodhound and go back where you came from. We don't need your kind of help."

"Now wait a minute," Tank began.

"It's all right, Sheriff," Lucky cut in. "I'm used to this." She reached for the woman's arm. "Really, ma'am, it's all right. If you could understand—"

The woman shrugged her off. "I understand we don't want that monster hounding our baby."

King approached the trio in the road. "Good morning, Mrs. Asbury," he said, flashing the boyish grin that always transformed his face. "Perhaps I can put your mind at ease." He took the woman's arm and steered her away from Lucky.

Clearly flattered by King's attention, Mrs. Asbury tugged at her sweater and watched his face closely while he talked. Lucky caught enough of

King's soft speech to know that he was explaining how the bloodhound got its ancient name, that it really meant only "blooded hound" as in *blue*-blood, and certainly did not mean that the dog scented on or had an appetite for blood. *Bless you, King,* she thought. She had no time for lengthy lectures to correct such misconceptions.

But as she turned back to the cruiser, she spotted a couple huddled in the backseat of the Asbury car.

"Amy's parents," Tank muttered beside her. "The Roberts."

Lucky strode over to the car. "Mr. and Mrs. Roberts? Please don't worry. Cosmo wouldn't hurt your little girl for anything."

"Find her, please," Mrs. Roberts said. "I'm sorry about my sister. She's upset. We're all upset. Please forgive her. Just find my baby, please. Please find my little Amy." The woman sobbed uncontrollably and buried her head on her husband's shoulder.

The father swallowed hard. "Please, officer . . . she's just a baby. So little. So little to be out there in the woods alone."

Lucky nodded. "I'm going to try very hard, Mr. Roberts. Believe me, if she can be found, Cosmo will find her. Right now he's the best chance she's got. Excuse me," she said in a rush. "I really must get started."

She blinked back tears and hurried back to Cosmo. After yesterday's experience, she braided her hair into a single pigtail down her back, and remembered King's remark that she looked like an Indian maiden. She pushed away the thought. Nothing must interfere with finding this child.

A stiff-billed cap would be more likely to stay on her head and afford some protection from tree branches and rain or snow. For a trail as long as this one might prove to be, she had brought her backpack. Removing her uniform necktie, she stuffed it into a side pocket of the pack. She double-checked for the small first-aid kit, a few sticks of beef jerky, a small box of raisins, some lemon drops, her hunting knife, a waterproof container of matches, and the Mylar emergency blanket.

While the deputy filled her canteen from a well in the campground, Lucky searched the sky. She was glad for the yellow rain slicker in her pack. *Never let it be said I don't learn from experience,* she thought as she exchanged the down vest for the slicker. Rain seemed likely at any moment.

And with fresh memories of their escape from the train, she decided to use the running belt. Though its width added bulk to her gun belt, walkie-talkie, and canteen, it left her hands free to fend off tree branches and manage the compass and map. A fastener from Cosmo's twenty-foot lead could also be released in an emergency. There were no freight trains in the woods, but other dangers almost certainly awaited her. Knots in the lead just below her waist and at one-foot intervals gave her a better grip on the nylon webbing.

She considered whether to carry her uniform coat, because it would probably be warmer in the woods out of the wind, and running behind Cosmo would warm her up in any case. But as unsettled as the weather seemed to be, she couldn't risk leaving the coat behind. Much as she dreaded the extra weight, she rolled both the coat and the down vest and stuffed them into her pack.

To get her bearings, she unfolded the large map of the national forest and spread it on the hood of the sheriff's car. Cosmo would lead the way, but she wanted some idea of the surrounding terrain. The topographical maps, because they were of much smaller areas, would be of no use until she knew where they were headed. Stepping away from the car, she checked her compass to verify her impression of directions, then buttoned both the instrument and the map into a shirt pocket.

She shouldered her backpack and smoothed on her tight-fitting deerskin gloves. When she buckled the trailing harness onto Cosmo, he knew she was ready to go to work, and his tail waved in anticipation.

"Ready, Sheriff?" Lucky turned to see that Tank had no pack of his own, but he had exchanged his finely tooled boots for heavy running shoes. Thick-soled hikers similar to her own would have been better.

To shield his Stetson from the rain, Tank had slipped over it a plastic covering, but to protect himself from the elements, he wore only a light-weight denim jacket over his uniform. Lucky started to protest his lack of foresight, and then thought better of it. A grown man and an officer of the law, he didn't need a mother hen and would surely resent one.

As Cosmo sniffed at Tank's trousers and growled softly, Lucky puzzled over the dog's behavior, but only briefly. There were more important things to worry about. She took the bag with Amy's clothing from the deputy and walked the dog out onto the gravel toward the footprint in the creek bank. Opening the bag of scent articles, she lowered it to Cosmo's level. "Cosmo, *find!*" she ordered.

The hound nosed the bag almost casually. His tail thumped once against Lucky's pants leg. The dog loved children, and she wondered if he had some way of knowing that their quarry was young and needed him desperately. The massive muscles in his shoulders and thighs bunched, and he strained against the coiled lead.

Lucky paid out the lead slightly. "Let's go, Cosmo!"

The dog seemed to test the air, then lowered his great head and swung it to swirl and collect the scent. Tail down, working slowly and carefully, Cosmo sought Army's most recent scent trail. He cast along the beach for a few paces, ignoring the roped-off footprint, then pivoted and tried the other direction. Back and forth along the shore he tacked, then turned toward the campground. Although Lucky had given him no indication as to which campsite was the springboard, he circled the lost child's camper and cast back and forth along the path leading from the camper to a public rest room.

Lucky shot a glance to where the sheriff stood, hands on hips. To an onlooker, she knew, there was no apparent change in Cosmo's attitude. Apparently relaxed and unhurried, he seemed to be merely wandering along, not working hard to find the scent.

"What about the footprint?" Tank called out without bothering to mask his impatience.

Lucky shook her head and concentrated on Cosmo. He had slowed now to isolate Army's scent among the many in the dry, sandy soil of the children's playground. "Come on, Cosmo, come on," she urged softly. "Let's go find that little girl. Come on." She pushed away the thought that Moonshine might have been off and running by now. The hounds were trained to follow the most recent trail of the scent. In this situation, where all the child's scents would be recent, that would take considerable discernment. She resolved to be patient.

A gust of wind whipped sand under the swings, and Cosmo shook his head and sneezed.

No telling where the wind has blown the scent,

Lucky thought with a groan. She darted a look at the sky, where dark clouds hung low and scudded among the hilltops. Conditions couldn't possibly be worse. She bit her lip and urged Cosmo on. He was already working hard, but her words of encouragement always seemed to help.

The dog circled the playground one last time and then headed back toward the camper, almost meandering. With dejection and disapproval apparent in his stance, Tank stood in a knot of men near the trailer. A small crowd had gathered near the parking area, and Lucky heard their laughter and few catcalls.

"Better watch out now, Tank. That there dog's liable to run you plumb to death!"

"We'll take care of things here whilst you're gone, Sheriff. That is, if you ever get gone!"

Then a muttering that Lucky didn't hear was greeted with raucous guffaws and hoots of ribald laughter. She caught only a snatch of something about a yellow slicker.

"Come on, Cosmo," she urged. "Come on, pick it up and let's go. Let's go to work." She hoped her own lack of confidence was not audible to him.

The bloodhound cast along the road around the circle of campsites, occasionally sidetracking to a tree or a tent. Campers watched his progress nervously, their faces reflecting a typical, unwarranted fear of the huge dog.

When Cosmo completed the circuit of the campsites and they came again into the view of the spectators around the sheriff, the laughter was general and louder.

Lucky kept her gaze on Cosmo, encouraging him softly and, although she was sure he was already doing his best, urging him to work harder.

"You know," she heard on the wind, "I wouldn't give you a dime for one of them bloodhounds."

Near the communal well the dog stopped abruptly, and blowing air through his nostrils in short bursts, he then inhaled deeply. Nose twitching, he left the road and seemed to wander aimlessly across an unoccupied campsite and toward the forest beyond.

The wind seemed less sharp on this side of the circle, broken by the press of trees and the few buildings serving the campground. Working around the empty campsite, Cosmo crossed a dim path almost hidden in the dense woods. Although still bare of new leaves, the trees crowded each other closely, the foot trail between them wide enough only for single file.

The wind dropped suddenly and a fine rain began to fall, as though the mists hovering over the hilltops had settled into the hollow. If Cosmo was ever going to find Amy's trail, it would be now.

Lucky resisted the urge to check her watch. It seemed a long time since she had scented Cosmo on the child's clothes, but probably only a few minutes had elapsed. Without raising her head, she glanced sidelong at the group of men near the creek. They had only assumed that the footprint in the creek bank was the lost child's, but many other children had access to this area. They might have wasted an entire day on a wild-goose chase.

As she watched, Cosmo nuzzled a pile of half-rotted leaves, turning them over with his nose and breathing deeply of their undersides. When he shook his head from side to side, his long ears swirled over the soil beneath them. He exhaled sharply and took a quick step, then another. His tail lifted slightly. Lucky recognized the signs. Cosmo had the trail!

Before she could call out to Tank, the bloodhound loped ahead. Trapped in the leaves underfoot, the scent must be fresh and strong. Cosmo rushed down the narrow path through the trees. Hard put to keep up, Lucky supposed that eventually Tank would realize what had happened and that someone had seen where they disappeared.

Wet and slimy, last autumn's leaves slid under her feet as Lucky hurried after the bloodhound. He scrambled up a slight incline as the narrow trail climbed the hillside. Lucky's gaze swept the occasional patches of bare ground. She was searching for a footprint. But the hard, rocky soil was undisturbed. There was no evidence that the child had passed this way, but the eager man-trailer strained at his harness and forced her into a near-run to keep up.

She had no time to dodge the tree limbs in her path and was grateful that her hands were free to protect her face. The wet slicker helped them to slide harmlessly off her arms. In a more relaxed moment she would have enjoyed the aroma of rain-soaked woods. The pungency of an occasional damp red cedar or pine punctuated the earthy essence, especially when she brushed their branches.

Lucky wished she had remembered to check her watch when Cosmo hit the trail. Time became a blur of fending off tree limbs, of trying to look where her feet were falling in order to avoid a turned ankle, and of straining to see through the rain where Cosmo was headed. She was glad for all those training laps around the track.

She tried to estimate the distance they had come from the campground. So far the trail had led into relatively gentle rolling hills, enabling them to cover the distance quickly. But as the terrain gradually became more rugged, Cosmo slowed. Just as the going was tough for them, so it had been for their quarry.

There was no assurance, however, that they followed exactly in the child's footsteps. Unlike tracking dogs that followed the quarry more or less precisely, the bloodhound trailed the individual's scent, wherever the wind had blown it. Where the threadlike path was protected from the wind, Cosmo worked quickly, but in the more open stretches of the trail, the wind had apparently scattered the scent. The dog left the path now and again to sniff out assurance that he was still headed correctly. Despite the side trips through wild blackberry bushes and other thorny brambles, Lucky was able to slow to a fast walk, look around them, and catch her breath.

A glance over her shoulder yielded no sign of Tank. Through the trees she saw that the hiking trail roughly traced the course of the creek she had seen at the campground, now far behind and below them. The trail stabbed deeper into the woods, and occasionally almost paralleled the stream through the narrow holes. It was a wonder that the toddler had come so far upstream, but there was the matter of the twenty-four-hour head start.

After cresting a hill, the path began to descend sharply toward the streambed in an almost canyonlike hollow. Lucky caught an occasional glimpse of tumbled boulders along a sliver of rocky beach. When they broke into the open from the gloom of the forest, she caught her breath in dismay— directly ahead was a pool of water surrounded on three sides by trees pressing to its shores.

Beyond the pool was a small campground with perhaps a half dozen empty sites. She glimpsed through the trees a narrow road that switched back and forth across the steep hillside, its hairpin curves winding beneath a spectacular sandstone bluff. No wonder the campground was deserted; it was accessible only to very few vehicles and to determined backpackers.

Once across the small clearing, she held her breath as Cosmo veered sharply to follow a narrow ledge along the shore, almost doubling back on the trail—although on the other side of the stream—as they circled the pool. Raindrops rippled the surface, shimmering emerald green under the leaden sky, but Lucky could see from the steep contours of the terrain that the pool must be very deep.

Shifting her gaze to the boulder-strewn shoreline ahead of them, she scanned it for signs of a fall. If the child had stumbled or decided to wade, the trail ended here, and it would take a diver to find her body.

Cosmo splashed into the water and Lucky caught her breath. She had learned from experience that water was no barrier to the bloodhound's nose. If the child had entered the lake, Cosmo knew it. But the dog lowered his great head to lap at the surface, his long ears floating free. After a moment he returned to his search for the suddenly elusive trail.

Lucky spoke to the dog and called a rest stop. She spread her map beside her on a rocky bench and tried to shelter it from the rain. A glance revealed that the emerald lake was known as Gunner Pool. At her feet Cosmo panted heavily, saliva dripping from his tongue. His eyes begged to be on the trail, and he whimpered softly, watching her every movement for signs of action.

The diminishing wind fluttered the edges of her map, and Lucky noted its direction. If it had prevailed yesterday, the scent might well be downhill from them. She made a mental note to try that possibility if Cosmo hadn't relocated the trail in a few minutes. As she cooled, the wind felt sharp and she shivered. When her heart slowed and ceased pounding in her ears, she noted the background sound of rushing water, as though of rapids or falls. But a glance along the stream visible between the hills disclosed neither. Gunner Pool quivered hypnotically in the rain.

Cosmo leaped to his feet, a growl rumbling in his throat. He turned to face the hillside they had just left, his hackles rising, hair bristling along his back. A twig snapped and echoed like a gunshot in the cup-shaped hollow. Lucky whirled to see Tank bursting through the underbrush. Where she had tried to slip between the tree limbs, Tank bulled his way through them. If this were a criminal case, their quarry would be warned well in advance of Tank's coming. He collapsed breathlessly beside her.

Lucky shifted her backpack and adjusted a strap. Her pigtail had become so saturated with rain that it wicked water down her back. She lifted the braid from the nape of her neck and coiled it under her cap. A glance at her watch confirmed that the morning was half gone and there was no more hope of finding the child than there had been at daybreak. "Cosmo, find!" she said to the eager dog.

Cosmo's tail indicated his approval of her return to work. He began to cast for the trail at the point where she had called the rest, lowering his great head and swirling his ears to cup the elusive scent toward his nose. Slowly he worked back and forth between the pool and the primitive campsites.

Tank said nothing until he caught his breath. Then he informed her, "This is a waste of time."

Lucky shook her head. "The trail is old, Tank, but if you knew how many kids this dog has found, you'd be more optimistic."

Tank sat with his hands propped on his thighs, the angle of his Stetson clearly indicating his disapproval. "Let's go back. Nobody will blame him for losing a trail this cold." His voice echoed in the hollow.

She studied Cosmo. His attitude was good, and the angle of his tail indicated that hopeful traces of the scent were still present. "He's still working," she told Tank. "He hasn't given up, so why should we? I'm just hoping he doesn't go near that water."

As though her words were prophecy, the bloodhound veered sharply back toward the pool. Tail up, he appeared to be on the scent strongly again rather than merely casting for it, and Lucky held her breath. But he led the way around the shoreline and started back downstream.

Tank said in disgust, "He's leading us on a wild-goose chase." He stood, hands on hips, as if awaiting her reply.

Lucky ignored him and wondered that she had ever found him mildly attractive. Away from his circle of admirers, he was vastly different.

Cosmo picked up the pace, and she broke into a jog. This time a child's life might depend upon Cosmo's insistence on speed.

"That dog is crazy. You can't get through that way," Tank shouted after them. "There's a dam across the creek at the end of the hollow."

Now he tells me, Lucky thought, and realized that the sound of rushing water had become louder. She grasped Cosmo's lead, attached to the harness around her waist, and reined him in, hand over hand, until he was only a few feet in front of her. All the while he struggled to advance, leaping from rock to rock to clear the water eddying into hollows in the solid rock underfoot. Glancing around them, she realized that they had entered a rocky canyon, its steep walls gradually funneling to the point where the dam backed up the creek to form the emerald pool. It didn't take an engineer to determine, from the steepness of the hills flanking them, that the dam was tall and the fall long. She and Cosmo would have to retrace their steps to escape the gorge.

But Cosmo fought her control and struggled to pull her deeper into the canyon, closer to the waterfall. Her foot slipped on wet stone, and she threw out an arm to steady herself against the rocky wall closing in on them. Aware of the slack in his lead, the dog surged ahead, dragging her after him.

"Lucky, stop!" Tank's voice was barely audible above the roar of the falls. "You can't get through there. The dam is clear across, and it's too deep."

She glanced up to see him standing above her on the rim of the gorge. *Some backup!* she fumed silently. If he were doing his job, he'd be behind her helping instead of allowing her to blunder into this situation.

She struggled to plant her feet, halt the dog, and gauge the distance to the falls. But Cosmo leaped ahead. Why was he so insistent on continuing? If there was no way around the falls, why did the trail continue to the very brink? Was it possible that the child had wandered into the same trap and continued unsuspectingly to her death?

Chapter Five

*A*s Cosmo's lead went slack, Lucky tore her gaze from the point where the water fell into space to the dog.

He had halted under a shelf of rock jutting from the sheer face of the gorge. Below it was a dry shelter cave the size of a small room. She ducked under the overhang and followed Cosmo into the cave.

Once inside she could stand upright under a low ceiling. A musty smell, as though of great age, filled the room carved by water into solid rock. Cosmo snuffled around the remains of a fire and nosed a soiled blanket nearby.

"Good dog, Cosmo," Lucky said around the lump in her throat. If he had not insisted on continuing, she would have turned back before discovering the cave. She had nearly violated the bloodhound handler's most important rule: *Trust your dog.*

There was no doubt that the child had been here. But so had someone else. A rusty coffeepot lay on

a rock near the ashes of the fire, and several ammunition boxes lined the rear wall. A quick examina-
tion confirmed her suspicion of nonperishable food
supplies. Someone either lived or spent considerable time here.

Cosmo looked up from his task and growled a
warning.

"Well, I'll be. . . ." Behind her Tank gave a low
whistle that echoed eerily. "What have we here?"
He almost shouted to be heard over the noise of
the waterfall.

Lucky shot him a glance. "I'm beginning to
think Amy didn't just wander away from that
campground." She watched Cosmo follow the
child's scent across the earthen floor. "Or else
someone prevented her return."

Tank gestured his dismissal of her suggestion.
"Oh, come on. Are you saying the kid was in
here?"

Lucky jerked her head to the bloodhound. "*He*
says so, and that's good enough for me. If you don't
believe him, I bet you could find a little footprint
in that deep dust in the corner."

He folded his arms across his chest and stood his
ground.

"I wondered how a three-year-old could get so
far so fast," Lucky said. "I think she was carried."

Tank snorted. "You mean your dog hasn't
spelled it all out for you?" He shook his head. "You
women." He lifted and resettled his plastic-

wrapped Stetson. "How do you know the dog didn't smell the food or the guy who's been here?"

She took a deep breath to control her anger. "The hound was scented on the child—period. Bigfoot could be roaming around in these hills and he'd still follow the child. Nothing and no one else. Not rabbits and not cavemen. The little girl was here."

"All right, all right." He spread his hands. "So now what? Are you ready to go back?"

Lucky shook her head. "I'm going where Cosmo leads as long as he has the trail." She shifted the weight of her backpack and readjusted the equipment at her waist. Fumbling in the pocket of her slicker for a lemon drop, she popped it into her mouth rather than take time for a drink from the canteen.

Satisfied that the child was no longer in the cave, Cosmo cast around the entrance for the direction she had taken when she left. He worked patiently across the damp earth and rocks. Lucky saw no reason to explain to Tank how the scent could be scattered by wind or by currents of air off the water.

Tank stood to one side, not bothering to conceal his impatience. He looked at his watch, then scanned the sky. His denim jacket was soaked, as were his canvas shoes.

And still it rained. Lucky tugged her cap bill lower on her forehead to shield her face. "Come on, Cosmo, let's get to work," she murmured to the dog. "Which way from here, boy? Come on, come on."

Tank muttered an oath and retraced his steps to leave the gorge by the way he had entered.

Cosmo snuffled his loose lips and surged forward. Lucky moved with him, only to realize they were once more headed for the precipice where the water poured over the dam. From the corner of her eye she glimpsed the water picking up speed, churning as it approached the brink. Cold spray from the falling water joined the rain on her face, and the roar of the falls filled her head. There was no time to disconnect the lead binding her to the dog or to shout a command. Cosmo's lunge caught her off balance, and she could only stumble helplessly after him.

But in an instant the bloodhound veered, and he headed not for the waterfall but for the rock barrier hemming them in the gorge. Seemingly on the very brink of the falls, a fold in the sheer stone wall now riveted the dog's attention. He lifted his head to gaze up the slit, but it was far too narrow to admit his bulky body.

In a few steps Lucky stood beside him, her knees rubbery. She grasped the knotted lead with both hands and readied herself for a new lunge toward the falls. But the hound stared up at the stone wall. He seemed convinced that the strongest scent led straight up its face.

Lucky put her hand on the damp stone in front

of her and leaned to peer into the thin fold of rock. Natural indentations every foot or so up the wall had collected spray from the falls to form miniature pools. Was it possible that, using these pockets in the stone for toeholds, someone could climb out of the gorge? Leaping and clawing at the rock above him, Cosmo seemed convinced that they could.

She reached out to one of the hollows and scooped out the water. Chiseled scars in the rock confirmed her suspicion; someone had enlarged the natural depressions in the stone to form the slenderest of steps. An agile person could scramble up the series of toeholds to within a few feet of the top, just over her head, and then haul himself up the remaining distance to escape the gorge. She might possibly be able to follow.

But Cosmo could not. Standing on his hind legs, the dog tested the air above him. His giant nose worked constantly, confirming the trail now out of his reach.

"What the heck are you doing down there?" Tank's shout came from directly over her head.

She glanced up and said, "Looks like our mysterious caveman has an emergency exit." She indicated the toeholds in the face of the rock.

Tank shook his head. "I can't hear you over the falls," he yelled.

Since the only way to resume the trail was to retrace their steps and pick it up on top of the rock wall, Lucky hauled Cosmo out of the gorge. Joining Tank, she explained their findings, and added, "Now do you believe me? There's no way the little girl could have left that cave, found those steps, and climbed out of that gorge by herself. Someone either picked her up at the campground or found her wandering in the woods, and then brought her here to the waterfall and carried her up these steps."

He shifted his Stetson. "Maybe your dog is following some other trail."

Lucky took a deep breath. "Tank, that just wouldn't happen," she said evenly. "If Cosmo says Amy was here, trust me, she was here." She removed her cap and slapped it against her thigh to scatter the rain water. She glanced around the circle of forest hemming them in the hollow. The gentle mist had become a determined rain; the rocky ground was growing spongy underfoot. "I don't like this, Tank. I think someone kidnapped that little girl."

She considered urging him to start other searchers from this area, and then abandoned the thought, because other people traipsing around in the woods would considerably lessen whatever chance Cosmo might have of trailing the kidnapper. There was little doubt, judging by what she had seen of the sheriff's forces, that she and Cosmo represented Amy's best chance. But what if she dropped of exhaustion or ran the willing bloodhound to death? If she failed because of her own weakness, she would only confirm the predictions of those waiting below, that a woman had no place in the woods, or as a cop.

Tank gave the exaggerated sigh of a patient adult explaining something to a pouting child. "But there's absolutely no evidence of kidnapping." He jerked his head to the cascading water. "Maybe the waterfall confused your dog."

She shook her head. "No." She tugged her hat firmly into place and grasped Cosmo's lead. Raising her voice to be heard over the falling water, she said forcefully, "I'm sticking with this trail, and if that child is still in these woods, we'll find her. You can do as you please, but I still need a backup." She looked up at him and batted her eyelids mockingly. "Surely you're not going to abandon a little ole helpless woman up here in the wilderness?"

He snorted. "Helpless, my foot." But as he searched her face, his eyes softened. "All right, I don't think your pooch knows up from down, but I'll stick with you awhile longer."

Aware of the dog's expectant and eager gaze on her face, Lucky nodded. "*Find,* Cosmo!" she said.

The bloodhound leaped into action. He struck the trail immediately and worked it excitedly, almost dragging Lucky after him into the woods. Behind her, Tank activated his walkie-talkie to report their whereabouts and the decision to press on.

A few steps from the stone ladder out of the gorge, Cosmo turned upstream. Judging by his concentration and determination to hurry, the scent was strong. Lucky wondered if their quarry had spent the night in the cave, which would account for the improvement in the trail of scent. If so, they might possibly have a chance of catching up, especially if Amy's abductor didn't know he was being followed.

She grimly considered her conviction of a kidnapping. Judging from the way Cosmo worked, the child was definitely being carried. He followed the creek upstream from Gunner Pool into a narrow ravine between two hills. As they climbed, they threaded their way among giant boulders washed into the creek at flood stage. Although they still followed the hiking trail that chose the easiest route up the hills and across the contours of the land, it had apparently seen much less use above the last campground. The trail was less distinct, harder to follow. She wasn't sure she could even stay with it if Cosmo were not dragging her along inexorably.

Lucky noticed that the stream was becoming swollen with rainwater and the runoff from the surrounding hills. And still it rained.

After topping a particularly punishing hilltop, she halted the dog and leaned her shoulder against a giant white oak to rest. Cosmo would follow the trail until he dropped, so she must think for both of them, to conserve their energy and strength for what might lie ahead.

From this vantage point she could see for miles. Here the cloud-crowned ridges were punctuated by peaked knobs and cut-off mountains deeply dissected by numerous creeks. The incredible scenery was so overwhelmingly beautiful that it brought tears to her eyes. Why had she ever left Arkansas? And why did Amy's abductor carry her into some of the wildest, least-populated terrain in the state? While it was true he might elude capture forever in such country, it could also be an inescapable prison of his own making.

Tank pulled up beside her, leaning on his thighs like a marathon runner. "Whew!" he puffed. "Don't you ever quit?"

She shook her head. "Cosmo would run his heart out to find that child. And I keep thinking of her half naked in the rain. But Cosmo and I can't keep this up indefinitely. We need another bloodhound team to work in relays."

"Forget it. There isn't another bloodhound available in three states. Don't take it so personally. There are searchers fanning out every direction from that campground, and as soon as the weather cooperates, there'll be choppers."

"Helicopters are no good in these dense woods, and you know it. As for foot searchers. . . ." She wanted to point out that they might have found the child the first day, but hadn't.

"Lucky, I gotta tell you—I don't think a three-year-old kid could have come this far. In fact, I don't think she would even have headed in this direction. The climb is too punishing and too rocky.

For all we know she was barefoot." He jerked his head to the dog. "And I don't have the faith in that animal that you seem to have. How do we know he's not trailing an innocent hiker or a poacher?"

Lucky looked him in the eye. "I tell you that isn't possible. Another breed might do that, but not a bloodhound. And you've just answered your own argument. A toddler couldn't possibly cover so much ground alone. Besides, a lost, wandering child would probably circle or backtrack or zigzag."

"Frankly, I think this is a waste of my time. I should be back at headquarters coordinating the search."

"Then go. But with or without you, I'm staying on the trail as long as Cosmo can find it." Without looking at him, she consulted her compass and hitched up her backpack. "Let's go, Cosmo, *find!*" she ordered, thinking of how different things would be if King were running backup.

As the rain continued, Cosmo worked more certainly and quickly, but that only increased Lucky's fatigue. She struggled to dismiss the ugly possibility raised by the sheriff, that of a false trail. The more tired she became, the more plausible it sounded, but if she lost faith in Cosmo now, she'd be going back on everything she had learned in her years of running bloodhounds.

In late afternoon they broke out of the trees into another primitive campground, smaller than the last, but with a clearing large enough to land a helicopter. Lucky collapsed on a log near the stream. Cosmo lapped the water and sank to his belly near her, panting heavily, his eyes sad.

"I'm so hungry I could eat a bear," Tank complained as he sprawled on a boulder nearby. "And thirsty."

Lucky shifted the lemon drop in her mouth. "Have a lemon drop? Better than nothing." Some instinct urged her to conserve the water in the canteen strapped to her belt.

He shook his head. "I'm just about ready to risk drinking that." He indicated the stream.

She studied the suffering hound. Although she had been warned long ago to avoid drinking any untreated water anywhere, the dog required large amounts of water, far more than she could carry, especially on such a trail as this one. Nor could she carry dog food. Though she could keep going for a while on lemon drops and raisins, Cosmo could not.

The rain had settled into a fine drizzle. She spread her map on the boulder and bent over it to afford it some protection from the damp.

Tank groaned and hauled himself upright. "This is where the hiking trail ends," he said. "Playtime is over. Now we'll separate the men from the boys, so to speak." He looked sidelong at her and suppressed a grin. He jabbed a finger at the map. "We're here at Barkshed, an old camp of the Civilian Conservation Corps. No matter which way we go from here, it's gonna be harder and slower." He sought her eyes. "Last stop for the chopper express to a steak dinner and a dry bed."

Lucky took a deep breath. "For the last time, Tank, I'm not quitting until the trail does." She glanced at the weary dog at her feet. "Or he gives out."

Tank radioed their position to headquarters, along with his opinion that they had followed a false trail.

But he was right about the difficulty awaiting them. In comparison, the trail so far had been relatively easy. Without the narrow track through the trees, Lucky fought grasping branches, sharp rocks underfoot, twisted roots that tripped and snagged. Cosmo slowed, exhaustion in his every glance. Darkness began to settle into the hollows.

And the bloodhound lost the trail. As the last of the daylight died, he cast desperately for the scent.

"Let's request a chopper while there's still light," Tank urged.

Lucky regarded him tiredly. "And land him where?" She circled a hand to indicate the thick forest surrounding them. "Besides, we might not be able to pick up the trail again in the morning. And in the meantime the kidnapper gets farther ahead of us."

"We can radio the coordinates of this spot."

She shook her head. "Amy needs us more than we need food and sleep. We'll stay here for a couple of hours to rest Cosmo, then move on."

Tank pivoted, kicked a tree, and muttered a string of curses. After a few moments he jerked his walkie-talkie from his belt and established a weak, staticky contact with his base. In response to the request for an explanation of their decision to stay in the forest, he mentioned Lucky's conviction that the child was being carried. His voice conveyed what his words could not, and those who listened would have no doubt he considered her a fool and a waste of his time.

He would abandon her if he could, Lucky conjectured, but he saw no way to do so without losing face with his men and his supporters. In their eyes, she was a helpless and misguided woman who needed Tank's protection.

She squatted to study the map by the fading twilight. Since leaving the last campground, the trail had veered westerly, but the general direction was still north and ahead was only more wilderness. All day they had followed the general course of Sylamore Creek, and just above their present location a small tributary joined the stream.

Standing behind her, Tank jabbed the map with a stick. "We're about here," he pointed out, as if assuming her incapable of determining their location. "I don't get it. If some guy did kidnap the kid, why is he heading for the Leatherwood Wilderness? Once you cross Push Mountain Road"—he pointed to the designation for a primitive road— "there's nothin' for miles." He tapped her shoulder. "I mean, I'm talking *wilderness*. And when you get through the Leatherwood, you're in the Buffalo National River holdings. Nothin' there but more woods and wilderness. So much for your kidnapping theory." But his smooth voice sounded genuinely puzzled.

Lucky shrugged. "Perhaps he's heading for the road, hoping to get a ride out of the area." She studied the map. "Or for one of these rivers." She pointed out the Buffalo and the White rivers on the map, their confluence near the point where the Buffalo National River lands joined the Ozark National Forest. "Maybe he has a boat."

Tank snorted. "Not likely." He poked at the map with his stick. "There's a bluff on both of these rivers along there that tops out at five hundred feet. Nobody but an eagle or a vulture would go near the edge of that thing. It's straight down to a riverbed full of solid rock and too shallow to dive." He shook his head. "No way." He traced the line of road on the map. "If he crosses Push Mountain Road, there's nothin' ahead but woods and wilds— and bein' trapped on the bluff."

"Maybe he has another cave hideout somewhere in the Leatherwood Wilderness. And maybe he doesn't know we're following him."

When Tank made no response and settled him-

self on the ground against a boulder, Lucky re-
folded and stowed the map. Now that she had
cooled, she donned her uniform coat over her down
vest and then scooped away the wet leaves and pine
needles under a grove of large pine trees. Unlike
the leafless deciduous trees around them, the pines
might afford some limited shelter from the rain.

Deciding to leave the dog's lead fastened to her
waist harness, she called Cosmo to her side and settled them both under the Mylar wrap from her
pack. Over it she spread her slicker to afford a little
more protection from the rain.

Cosmo's usual worried look seemed more pro-
nounced, as though he only reluctantly consented
to rest with a trail unresolved. He leaned against
her and slowly slid into a prone position, resting
his droopy jowls on her thigh. She removed her
gloves and rewarded him with petting and affection
for a hard day's work. In a pocket of her down vest
she found a dog treat she used for rewards when
training. He took it eagerly, and she wished there
were more.

In a few moments they were warm and comfortable, in contrast to Tank's sodden denim jacket and
sorry plastic-covered hat. She shared her jerky with
Cosmo and offered some to Tank. He refused.

His discomfort increased as the darkness deepened and the temperature dropped. Lucky watched
him struggle with stubborn male pride. At last,

teeth chattering, he said, "How about sharing some of that blanket with me?"

Lucky suppressed a smile and nodded. "Sure." She lifted one edge, aware of what it had cost him to admit defeat. More serious, he was in real danger from exposure.

As Tank approached them, Cosmo lifted his nose and growled a warning. Shivering, Tank crossed to Lucky's opposite side and crawled under their coverings. Lucky put an arm around the dog's neck. "It's all right, boy," she murmured.

Cosmo subsided, but shifted his position so that he could watch Tank's face. Even when his eyes drooped shut, he jerked awake with Tank's every movement.

Having noticed no protective instinct in the bloodhound previously, Lucky marveled at his behavior. And she remembered that the dog had correctly sized up this man some hours before her own belated recognition.

She squirmed for a comfortable position on the damp ground, and thought about Amy, probably cold and wet and terrified. She pushed away the image. It would be better not to become emotionally involved. If she did only her job, both she and the child would probably be better off.

Tank pressed closer to her and ignored Cosmo's low warning.

In spite of her decision not to dwell on Amy,

Lucky wondered if the kidnapper had harmed her. She took a deep breath and repressed the thought.

To avoid the insistent worry about Amy, Lucky allowed it to be replaced by the memory of King's handling of the Asbury woman at the campground. She had forgotten how easily he controlled any situation, how commanding his physical presence was.

She quickly rejected that line of thought too, and sighed.

Tank slipped an arm around her shoulders and pulled her closer. "Don't worry, honey. We'll find her," he said.

Lucky stiffened and jerked away from him. "I would have bet a million dollars that you'd try something sooner or later." She resisted an urge to slap him. "Get away. Get out from under my blanket." Cosmo growled his reinforcement of her command.

Tank blinked. "What? What did I do? I was just trying to comfort you." He didn't budge. "We will find her, you know. We'll find her safe and sound."

"You weasel. Quit trying to change the subject. And there's no guarantee we'll find her, safe or otherwise. This is the real world, Sheriff, not your playacting at law enforcement. Little girls do disappear and sometimes—" She broke off and lowered her voice. "Get away from me."

"Aw, Lucky, I'll freeze to death! I'm soaked to the skin." He regarded her from under the dripping brim of his Stetson. "I thought you needed a backup so darned bad."

The rain had intensified to a steady, soaking downpour that filtered through the pines overhead and pattered around them in the darkness. "All right, you can stay," she said. "But if you touch me again, I'll give you a karate chop that'll have you waking up sometime next week." She settled back against the tree trunk well away from him. Cosmo growled his disapproval of her decision.

Tank turned away from Lucky and the dog, and in a few minutes his snores rivaled the splash of the rain in the pines.

Lucky allowed her head to sink against the rough bark of the pine tree behind her. She realized that she had been only vaguely aware of her fatigue until she rested. Now it washed over her in waves and seemed to weigh her limbs to the ground. Sleep was out of the question for fear they would stay too long off the trail, but she must close her eyes, if only for a few minutes.

She awoke with a start, struggled with disorientation and guilt for a moment, and then became aware of Cosmo's agitation. On his feet, his great head near hers, he pawed at her arm and whimpered. When she looked at him in surprise, barely able to discern his face in the darkness and the pelting rain, his eyes searched hers and he nudged her with his nose.

Over Cosmo's whine of distress, Lucky became aware of another sound, a roar that grew louder even as she tried to identify it. It was much too loud to be wind in the trees. A tornado? Conditions didn't seem appropriate for such a violent storm. A helicopter? Surely not, not in this weather at night. Then what was it?

Cosmo left her side, ran to the length of his lead, and struggled against it, leaping and charging away from her, lunging against the nylon strap binding them.

Lucky's mind raced. Whatever had come over the dog, his desperation to leave this spot was abundantly clear. She stumbled stiffly to her feet and shook Tank to wake him. As she did so, the truth dawned. "Wake up, Tank!" she cried. "Flash flood!"

Entangled in the blanket, slicker, and Cosmo's lead, Lucky could not move. She snatched at them, wadding them under her arm to free her feet. The cold rain pelted the back of her neck and trickled under her collar to roll down her back. She ignored it. There might be only moments before the thundering wall of water was upon them.

She had seen huge boulders tumbled by such floods, had watched grown trees ripped out by the roots, cars full of people swept away like a child's toy. She had seen at first hand the devastation and death wreaked by a gentle mountain stream so swelled by runoff from the steep hillsides that it rampaged its way down the valley.

"Run!" she shouted to Tank, who watched in bewilderment her efforts to stand as Cosmo lunged wildly at the far end of his lead. She snatched up her backpack and hooked it over an elbow. "Flash flood!"

Tank's eyes grew wide and white in the darkness. Scrambling to his feet, he charged away from her, straight for the flooding creek.

"This way!" she screamed over the roar of the approaching water. She grasped Cosmo's lead to help brace herself against his lunges, and she struggled to withstand his determination to reach higher ground.

Tank ignored her shouts of warning and plunged into the woods toward certain death.

Lucky hauled on Cosmo's lead with both hands to pull him after her and staggered after Tank. She plucked at his jacket, then grasped his arm and held on tightly. "Wrong way!" she shrieked. "You're heading toward the creek! We've got to go *that* way!" She jerked her head behind her. "And we've got to get to higher ground *now.*" Partly to make herself heard over the deafening rumble of the approaching flood and partly to penetrate the panic she saw mirrored in his wild eyes, she stood on tiptoe to scream into his face. "*This* way! Follow me!"

Still grasping Tank's jacket, she whirled and

stumbled after Cosmo, the plunging bloodhound impelling her to run to keep from being dragged. She lost her grip on Tank's sleeve and darted a glance over her shoulder. If he did not follow, he was doomed. Maybe it was already too late.

But Tank stumbled after them. Then, with but a few strides of his long legs, he passed them by without a backward glance.

In the darkness Lucky tripped over a tree root and sprawled in the mud. Cosmo's leaps dragged her a few feet until she managed to grasp the trunk of a tree in her path. The dog barked his impatience. Sharing his desperation, Lucky scrambled to her feet to be towed along by the lead fastened to her waist harness.

The hillside under her feet tilted sharply, too steep for her to stand upright. She clawed upward on all fours, half climbing and half dragged. Her gloveless hands encountered thorns and rasping stones. And all the while she knew they were still too low to escape the flood.

Chapter Six

*T*he awful sound of the coming torrent filled Lucky's head. The ground beneath her trembled as a crash of thunder swelled the roar. In her mind's eye the wall of water swept down the creek bed toward them, pushing ahead of it rocks and logs and other debris from which there would be no mercy. Though certain that they had camped well away from the stream, Lucky felt equally sure that it was not far enough to escape the surging flood.

She struggled to stand. But the desperate lunges of the one-hundred-pound dog on the other end of the lead made it impossible to get her balance on the steep pitch of the hillside. She fell heavily and slid backward on the slippery ground underfoot, then floundered hand over hand through the mud churned by the driving rain. The backpack, dangling by its strap over her arm, dragged and caught on every tree root and rock. Her coat and blanket tangled in the lead and further impeded her progress, but defied her efforts to abandon them. Cosmo plunged and leaped against her weight on the lead, but was unable to tow her up the slope.

It was no use. She thought of King. If he had been her backup . . . or if she had married him five years ago. . . .

Lucky rolled onto her side and fumbled for the catch on the belt around her waist. If she could reach and release it, Cosmo would be free to save himself. But the struggling dog kept the nylon strap taut and straining, and without slack in the lead she could not manipulate the ring that had been designed to prevent accidental opening. There was little hope of releasing the catch in the darkness, even if she were able to ease the tension on the lead.

Renewing her efforts to clamber up the hillside, Lucky pushed with her feet while grasping with her hands, her knees pressing against the ground to hold every hard-won inch of gain. But even as she wallowed upward, she knew she was running out of time. Although she could not see it, the wall of water was rushing toward them.

"Give me your hand!" Tank cried.

Lucky looked up and searched for him somewhere above her in the darkness. But the rain pummeled her eyes to slits; only the panic rising in her throat prevented her from crying out.

"Give me your hand!" Tank repeated hoarsely, and this time his grasping hand closed around her wrist.

She gripped his arm with both hands. Blinded

by the tangled mass of coat and blanket and the dangling backpack still hooked over her arm, she pushed with her feet and clung desperately to Tank's arm.

In a flash of lightning she glimpsed Tank above her. He leaned precariously over the edge of a rocky shelf jutting from the hillside. His other arm hugged the trunk of an old cedar apparently growing in solid stone. At the end of his taut lead, Cosmo crouched beside him, the dog's face reflecting his understanding of Tank's struggle to save her.

With Tank holding her in an upright position, Lucky managed stiff-legged giant steps up the almost perpendicular hillside. Tank shifted his weight farther onto the ledge; his improved leverage enabled him to almost lift her free of the ground. Both Tank and the tree appeared to have only tenuous holds on the rock. Lucky prayed that the tree, after clinging to that rock for maybe a hundred years, could withstand their weight under the onslaught of the rain.

"Grab the tree trunk!" Tank shouted when she hung directly below him and the ledge. "Grab the tree and hang on!" As if reinforcing the command, Cosmo barked sharply.

Lucky feared letting go of Tank's arm, but she swung against the ledge and grabbed for the tree with one hand.

"Hang on tight!" Tank yelled against her ear. "Here comes the water!"

She fought the urge to look down and wrapped her arms around the trunk of the ancient cedar, her legs dangling below the ledge. The incredible roar of the approaching flood drowned even the hammering of her heart in her head. Thundering only feet below her, a mountain of debris rode high on the crest of a wall of water like a tidal wave.

Tank released his hold on the tree to grasp the lead still fastened to the belt around her waist. For a moment her weight almost pulled him over the edge of the shelf, but slowly, hand over hand, he hauled her closer to him until at last he could grip the waist harness itself. Clambering to his knees, he gave a mighty heave and rolled her body onto the ledge beside him just as the flood waters slammed at the spot where she had hung only an instant before. Then he scrambled across the ledge and hunkered against the hillside behind them.

Oblivious of the rain, Lucky clung to the rough wet stone under her and fought for control of her breathing. Cosmo pawed at her shoulder. Only inches below them the flood thundered past, filling the little valley where they had rested, ripping at the pines and clawing at their rocky perch. The old cedar quivered under its onslaught. If only the stone outcropping, which must have survived many such floods, could withstand just one more, they were safe.

She stared numbly into the darkness. In the intermittent flashes of lightning she caught glimpses of uprooted trees, boulders the size of houses, tangles of debris, all borne on the flood, flashing by her perch at unbelievable speed. The serene Ozark stream, with its gentle pace and crystal-clear water, was only a dreamlike memory. Now the roiling water was thick, choked with the soil sluiced off the hillsides by the downpour along its course, especially from far upstream where the hills were even steeper and the runoff faster.

Dimly aware of the smell of wet dog, Lucky sat up, reached a trembling hand to the bloodhound, and hugged him to her side. Though she could not hear his whimper over the chaos of the flood, she felt it in his throat. She murmured reassurance and praise near a muddy ear. If it were not for Cosmo's warning and Tank's help, she would have been washed away like a leaf.

Under her the ledge shuddered, reminding her their haven was only temporary. She knew that the outcropping was vulnerable to the gnawing and hammering action of the rampaging water. Though the rain had stopped, at least for the moment, it might still be raining upstream. In any event, runoff would continue for hours and the flood could worsen.

She turned to peer into the darkness behind her. Only Tank's Stetson was dimly visible until the flash of distant lightning illuminated his huddled form. He cradled the elbow of his left arm in his right hand; his face was drawn in pain and fear.

"Tank?" she said, and realizing he could not hear, she crawled across the ledge to his side. Cosmo followed, his lead slack. "Tank?" she shouted, her face near his. "Are you hurt?" She gently touched his arm.

He turned his head so that his mouth was near her ear. "Dislocated my shoulder," he shouted. "Or broke it. I think we need to make for higher ground."

"Right." But she wondered how he would climb with only one good arm. Though he had given no sign, he must have injured his shoulder while hauling her onto the ledge. His heroism in saving her life might yet cost him his own.

Hurriedly she stuffed the blanket and coat into the backpack and shrugged through the straps. Tank needed a sling for his arm, but it would have to wait until they were on higher, safer ground. She gathered in Cosmo's lead until the dog stood at her side where his weight and strength could help tow her up the hillside. "Let's go," she said.

Tank rose awkwardly to his feet but shook off Lucky's helping hand. Still cradling his injured arm in the palm of his other hand, he jerked his head toward the hillside. "You lead."

Lucky peered above her. Though it was still dark, the approaching dawn seemed to backlight the sky. The densely wooded hillside appeared less steep above the ledge; with effort they would be able to climb it standing up. Below her, the seething flood reflected the first tentative light and gleamed like a river of molten metal. The sound of its passing seemed to penetrate her being. "Heel, Cosmo!" she shouted, and moved off the outcropping onto the hill itself.

She allowed Cosmo to take a slight lead and lean into his harness, towing her after him up the steep slope. "Take my arm," she yelled to Tank in an effort to assist his laborious progress.

He shook her off, and with his good hand he grasped the branches of trees to steady himself and to keep from slipping backward.

As she climbed, Lucky searched the ground in the graying light for evidence of past floods. Once well above the last shelf of debris and driftwood, she called a halt, and dropping the pack, she allowed her trembling legs to buckle and she sprawled on the rocky ground. Panting heavily, Cosmo lay on his side near her. Tank collapsed against a nearby tree.

After a long while, the dawn overcame the darkness of both night and clouds to reveal that the flood had indeed swallowed their rescue ledge. She shuddered when she saw that, as she'd feared, the torrent had crept up the hill behind them. If Tank had been too badly injured to move from that rock, she might have had to choose between perishing with him or leaving him to die alone, swept away by the incredible force of the flood. She shook her head and pushed the thought from her mind. While such a quandary deserved pondering for the sake of her own self-knowledge, this was not the time.

Equally unwelcome were the persistent thoughts of King and of his expertise in first-aid treatment, of his ability to move quickly and safely through the wilderness, of his strength and gentleness.

Lucky shoved away such wishful thinking. Amy was still out there somewhere, if spared by the flood, and the child needed her and Cosmo. Now their work would be doubly difficult if not doubly dangerous. The scent in the valley had no doubt been swept away by the flood. Picking up the remnant of a trail could prove impossible for the dog.

And obviously she had lost her backup. As she fashioned a makeshift sling from the Mylar blanket, she studied Tank in the dim light. His face drawn in pain, he huddled against the tree, the big Stetson lowered almost to his knees.

She cleared her throat. "Do you want to radio for the chopper, or shall I?"

He straightened and shot her a sharp glance. "I can do it," he said, and fumbled with his good hand for the radio on his belt. She resisted the urge to extend a helping hand and reached instead for the map in her shirt pocket. Holding it close in the feeble light, she saw that Push Mountain Road, skirting the Leatherwood Wilderness, was probably the only possible pickup point. She told Tank, "Looks like there's an old logging road above us that comes out on Push Mountain Road below Cap Fork. Probably your best bet. It's well above the flood."

There was no hope of returning to Barkshed camp across the swollen creek. Even when the flood waters fell, perhaps hours hence, the current would be too swift to ford. "It's maybe two hours to Push Mountain Road, depending on the terrain," she said. "Can you make it?" She knew he had little choice. The helicopter could not land in the dense forest, nor could he climb a rope ladder they might otherwise lower to him. And if he waited for a rescue team to reach him with a stretcher and carry him out, it would be hours before he received medical care.

Tank nodded even as he established contact with his base. With a few words of explanation he arranged for the pickup, shouting to be heard above the flood and the out-of-range static. Only their altitude permitted any contact at all.

Lucky studied the map. They had outrun their radio contact with headquarters, and Cosmo's only hope of picking up Amy's trail lay in her ability as a cop. Since it was likely that the kidnapper, or whoever carried the child, was on the other side of the flooded Bee Branch Creek, there was little to be gained by wasting the time it would take to search only this side of the stream. Chances were that their quarry was also heading for Push Mountain Road. The only reasonable course of action was for her to escort Tank there to meet the helicopter, then cast up and down the road in the optimistic hope of picking up the child's scent.

The forest around them began to awaken; though barely audible over the roar of the flood, birdsong greeted the dawn and the signs of spring, including the swollen stream. On the map, she noticed a Forest Service road north of Bee Branch that led from Barkshed camp to Push Mountain Road. Roughly parallel to their own planned route, it was on the opposite ridge, across the flooded branch.

With a flash of certainty she knew that their quarry would strike it while fleeing from the flood. In fact, the odds were that he was familiar with the national forest and knew about the wilderness road. If he reasoned at all, he would likely assume that his pursuers, if indeed he was aware of them, were far enough behind him to be cut off by the flood. He would take the easier route and follow the road to its junction with Push Mountain Road. That backwoods intersection was not far north of where the helicopter would pick up Tank.

With just a little more luck, and if she was right about the kidnapper's heading for the Leatherwood Wilderness and the rivers beyond, Cosmo would pick up Amy's scent where the man carried her across Push Mountain Road. Lucky carefully folded and pocketed the map. She took a deep breath of air perfumed by damp leaves and rotting wood. If she was wrong, then it would be the end of the trail for Cosmo and her. The crackle of Tank's radio disturbed her concentration.

"It's storming there now," he reported, "but they'll take off as soon as they can and meet us on Push Mountain Road about a mile north of where the old logging road comes out. The road's too narrow for the chopper anywhere else. Cap Fork's flooded too. We can't cross it, so we'll have to leave the road there and cut across country along the ridge to Push Mountain." He winced with pain as he settled back against the tree. With his good hand he pushed back his Stetson, and he tried a grin as he said, "Once I get this thing taken care of, I'd like to buy you breakfast. You're one heck of a woman."

Lucky grimaced. "Thanks, Sheriff, but I'm going on. That little girl still needs me."

"That little girl is either dead from exposure or drowned in the flood!" he shouted. "You'll only kill yourself and your dog if you don't know when to quit."

She shook her head and met his eyes. "Maybe, but that's my job. Cosmo and I won't give up until your people either produce Amy or her body. As long as there's any hope at all, we're going on."

"With no backup? I thought regulations insisted that you have a backup." He cradled his injured arm and leaned forward to study her face.

"That's right, but this isn't a textbook case. Des-

perate circumstances call for desperate measures."
Working alone was indeed a breach of procedure,
especially in unfamiliar territory, but the missing
toddler was more important than her own safety.
She dropped her gaze, remembering that only a
short time ago her requisite backup had probably
saved her life. "We're going on," she added.

According to the map, the old lumber road could
support four-wheel-drive vehicles, but it was more
of a trail than a road. Little more than a grassy
opening between the dense trees, barely wide
enough to accept a lone Jeep, the track followed
the ridge above Bee Branch so that the sound of
the flooded creek below them constantly reminded
Lucky of their close encounter with death. But tree
branches formed a canopy overhead, and she
thought how pleasantly green and shady the route
would be in late spring and summer. Here and
there a young tree had sprouted along traces of the
old tire tracks. Nature certainly worked to reclaim
her own. Though she could not see it through the
trees and the gathering fog, she knew that the view
from this high ridge must be spectacular. They
were in the midst of some of the wildest country
in Arkansas, its ruggedness inhibiting human set-
tlement.

In spite of the mist and fog that swirled up from
the hollows below them, the former road provided
by far the quickest and easiest going they'd had
since leaving Blanchard Springs. Lucky dared to

hope that she and Cosmo might yet catch up with their quarry.

His tail between his legs, the bloodhound walked listlessly at her side, long ears swinging. His wrinkly brow drooped nearly over his eyes as his head hung in the dejection of an incompleted trail. But at least the flood had provided them both with some much-needed rest.

She ate the last of the raisins and jerky, and though thirsty, she settled for a lemon drop in order to save the little water left in her canteen for the dog.

By the time they reached the helicopter rendezvous, Lucky had decided that there was no need to spend precious time waiting with Tank for the chopper. She shook his hand and tried to express her thanks for his having saved her life. Then she gave him a quick hug before turning back to Cosmo.

"Go to work, boy," she said, reminding the dog they were still on the trail. But as she trudged after the bloodhound casting for the scent, she began to have doubts that the kidnapper would cross Push Mountain Road in this vicinity. And even if he did, there was no assurance that he would still be carrying Amy. Cosmo was scented on the child; he would ignore the scent of anyone else.

While it was simple enough to dismiss regulations that were not written to cover such a case as this, or even her own safety, she could not so easily ignore doubts of her ability. If she were really the cop—and the bloodhound handler—she had believed herself to be, she would not have been surprised by a flash flood in hilly country in rainy weather.

And if the dog did succeed in regaining the trail, could she keep up with him? Even the present relatively easy going of the gravel road skirting the wilderness seemed impossibly tiring. Despite her rest while awaiting the dawn, the ordeal of escaping the flash flood, heaped upon the fatigue of yesterday, weighed upon her. She was cold and wet, and nearly faint from hunger. Would her body be equal to the demands of a trail that would no doubt exhaust a stronger male? Did she have the right to endanger Amy's life further by proceeding, instead of insisting on a fresh search team with a physically stronger male handler? Most of all, was she truly dedicated to finding the child or did she persevere merely to prove a point to her sergeant? Or to Tank? Or, she admitted reluctantly, to King?

Pines crowded all around her, their branches meeting over the narrow track through the forest. Only the fact that it had been graded and graveled gave it the map's distinction of "road" rather than "trail." Judging by the size of the hardwoods pressing around her, these remote mountains had even escaped the turn-of-the-century exploitation by the loggers who had cleared so many other tracts. Although now regrown, the trees elsewhere were often of a fifty-year size rather than of centuries.

It was the replanting of those forests that had inspired King to enter the field of forestry, she remembered with a pang. How he must love this nearly untouched wilderness. For the hundredth time she pushed away thoughts of King. Her mission demanded her complete concentration.

Stumbling after the bloodhound, Lucky began to wonder whether she should disconnect herself from his lead; perhaps the waist harness was not a workable alternative. After all, he had nearly dragged her over the falls at Gunner Pool. On the other hand, she probably wouldn't have escaped the flood without his hauling her up the hill after him. More important, she had lost her gloves in the scramble from the flood. She inspected her hands. Covered with cuts and scratches from her clawing up the slope from the stream, they were in poor condition to handle the lead of a plunging bloodhound.

She studied the dog's efforts to find the trail. Superbly adapted and bred to do one thing and to do it better than anyone or anything else, Cosmo suffered from no distractions, no misgivings, no self-doubt. He did the work for which he was trained. Could *she* say the same?

But by the time they approached the junction with the grassy forest road where she hoped to resume the trail, the respite from struggling with the forest had provided some relief from her fatigue.

"Okay, heads up," she said, as much to herself as to Cosmo. If her luck held and if her police work was accurate, the kidnapper had come along that road to join theirs. She watched Cosmo closely. "What'cha say, boy, anything yet?" she crooned in encouragement. He seemed to tense as they neared the intersection.

A fine mist began to fall and she was about to trade her muddy coat for the slicker, when Cosmo's tail jerked stiffly upright. Like a signal flag, it told her he had struck the trail of Amy's scent.

Lucky dismissed as premature the urge to exult in her detective work, and she broke into a lope to keep up with the bloodhound, whose easy pace suggested that they must be close behind their quarry.

For more than two miles they followed the twists and turns of pine-and-maple-fringed Push Mountain Road. Occasionally, through gaps in the trees, she caught a glimpse of the hills around them, their rounded or peaked summits rising above the fog like scaly ridges along the spine of a dinosaur. Around every curve and over every rise Lucky expected to spot the man with Amy.

But by climbing Push Mountain they ascended into the low-hanging clouds. Fog and mist swirled across the road like smoke. Visibility became so limited that Lucky began to worry about bumping into the kidnapper without warning.

At the top of the mountain she strained to see the lookout tower indicated on the map, and she finally spotted the Forest Service gate across the graveled drive to the tower. But only the tall fence surrounding the tower and the first few feet of its four immense legs were visible. Above the barbed wire topping the fence, the rest of the giant structure disappeared into the fog like Jack's beanstalk.

A small sign on the fence said that the official National Forest Wilderness was closed to motor vehicles and motorized equipment. There would be no more logging roads, no helicopter clearings. Parked in a grove of oak trees beneath the tower was a Forest Service pickup, and Lucky wondered at the errand of the absent ranger. Whatever it was, she hoped he stayed out of Cosmo's way.

The bloodhound plunged ahead impatiently. Torn between her desire to recover Amy and her fear of running into the kidnapper unprepared, Lucky struggled to hold the dog to a manageable speed that would allow her to take evasive action if necessary.

As she hurried after him down the north side of Push Mountain, she peered into the fog-shrouded forest, from which branches reached into the road like claws. At the foot of the hill Cosmo plunged off the graveled trail and into trees even denser than before.

It was darker and quieter in the woods, and the fog enveloped them like cotton. But Lucky breathed in the familiar earthy aroma and felt less vulnerable than she'd been on the road. Because these trees were larger and more mature, there were fewer low-hanging branches to rake her face and tear at her clothing. Their quarry was avoiding the brushier areas. And thanks to a thick carpet of wet leaves and humus underfoot, it was easier going.

The trail climbed to a high ridge. The kidnapper had woods savvy, Lucky admitted. By staying out of the hollows and away from the dozens of streams that had carved the rugged terrain, he could avoid possible flash floods.

Cosmo slowed, but encountered no real difficulty. Trapped in the leaves and weighted down by the fine rain, the scent was easily detected, though more elusive than it had been on the road. For the moment at least, the bloodhound was content with a fast walk, which gave Lucky time to consider how best to approach the kidnapper. Much depended upon whether he was armed, and her first task would be to determine that. Amy's safety was the overriding consideration, of course, but if there were any way to manage it, she also intended to arrest the man.

She caught her breath at the sight of a dogwood tree in full bloom. Looming out of the mist beneath the canopy of tall oaks and pines, it seemed to glow with a light of its own, like a candle in the forest gloom. And it made her think of King.

Her thoughts were interrupted by the distant vibration of a helicopter. Relieved to know that Tank was safe, Lucky pushed away the memories of King with a promise to herself to reconsider them at a more appropriate time.

The roar of the chopper intensified, and the rhythm of its rotors beat in her head. Instinctively Lucky glanced upward, but she could see little but fog and the tangle of branches overhead. The machine must be above the clouds. Presently she realized that it was circling, spiraling over the mountaintop as though in a search pattern. Her heart leaped. Had they spotted something from the air? More likely, she realized immediately, they were looking for her, though there was as little chance they could see her through the trees and the fog as they could the kidnapper. No doubt Tank still thought she was crazy for resuming the search, and hoped to convince her to give up.

With a shock of guilt she remembered the radio strapped to her belt. A good police officer, ever mindful of the need for communication, would have switched it on immediately after leaving Tank. If the chopper was trying to contact her and couldn't raise her on the radio, they would assume she was in trouble.

Reluctant to halt the bloodhound, who had quickened his pace to a trot, Lucky fumbled at her belt for the radio. She glanced down and unsnapped the case, but before her fingers had closed over the instrument, she knew it was useless. The battery-indicator light was dark, and whether exhausted or damaged, there was no radio without the battery. There could be no contact with the outside world, no rescue in case of trouble or injury, no way to call in the troops if—when—she did find the child. What was worse, Tank might send searchers in after her, manpower that should not be diverted from the hunt for Amy.

She weighed the alternatives. Good police procedure and common sense said it was foolhardy to continue into the wilderness in bad weather with no provisions, no backup, and no radio contact with support personnel. But she knew there was no way she could go down the mountain and tell Amy's mother that she had quit when the bloodhound was trailing well, that she hadn't found her little girl because of a dead battery.

The thrumming of the helicopter faded away. She took a deep breath and broke into a jog to keep up with Cosmo. The dog's tail stood erect, indicating that he was pleased with the trail. They were gaining, the scent was good; she would not quit when Amy might be only moments ahead of them.

Tank knew which way she had planned to go. She must simply be extra careful. She concentrated on scanning the ground ahead in order to avoid rocks or tree roots that might trip her or cause a sprained ankle. She and Cosmo were truly on their own.

And one more thing was for sure. If she'd ever had any hope that the kidnapper was unaware of his pursuers, the chopper had blown that chance.

A fog-muffled sound intruded. Reluctant to stop the bloodhound, straining to hear above the noise of their progress, Lucky worked to identify the source.

Someone was following them. Had the kidnapper doubled back to check his trail? Cosmo would pay him no heed; he trailed only Amy. Lucky turned her head as far as she dared and listened intently. Someone or something was moving confidently through the woods behind her.

She held her breath. No, he was off to the downhill side, and it sounded as if he was moving quickly and surely at an angle to her own track. Whoever it was, he intended to head her off.

Chapter Seven

*A*s Lucky approached the next hollow, she realized how completely the fog had obscured her track. Visibility was no more than a few steps in any direction. Tree branches loomed in her path almost too late to avoid them. It might as well be Bigfoot heading for them; she wouldn't know it until he was on top of them.

Her choices were few. There was no place to run or hide, and he would hear her movements as easily as she heard his. She might choose the best nearby place to stop and make a stand. But that would mean halting Cosmo from Amy's trail. His tail stiffly erect, the dog leaned into his harness and pulled for every inch of slack in the lead.

Turning almost sideways to slip this way and that through the dense trees, she quickened her pace. And below them in the hollow, their pursuer quickened his.

But suddenly Lucky knew. She could not have said how she knew, whether from the length of his stride, or the timing of his footfalls, or the ease of his progress through the heavy timber. Or simply his nearness. It was King.

Giddy relief washed over her, followed immediately by an awareness of her appearance. The mist had saturated and penetrated her cap, pasting her hair to her head. Damp and dirty, her uniform probably smelled as unpleasant as it felt. She clutched her coat, muddied in the escape from the flash flood, and realized that her fingernails were rimmed by dirt.

Seeming to materialize out of the fog, King stepped into her path. His green eyes glowed like emeralds in the fog. Cosmo glanced up at him but never broke his stride. The dog seemed to grin, and Lucky saw recognition and acceptance in his eyes.

Lowering her eyes lest he see her thoughts, Lucky pretended to pick her steps on the pine-needled ground. She slowed to a fast walk and King fell into step beside her. Dressed for the trail, he wore a waterproof camouflage jacket and hiking boots. Strapped to the belt of heavy trousers designed to ward off brambles, thorns, and snakes were his radio and a canteen. A tall backpack rode between his shoulders.

When he said nothing after a few paces, Lucky shot him a glance.

From under the brim of his camouflage bill cap, his eyes met hers. He lifted an eyebrow and said, "Lose your walkie?" Though low and urgent, his voice was not breathless. He wasn't even slightly winded by his climb up the ridge.

Lucky shook her head. "Dead battery," she managed to say around the lump in her throat. His sudden presence had left her no time to prepare for the encounter.

"The child was kidnapped, just like you told Tank. We got a ransom call at headquarters just before I left." He flicked a glance at Cosmo, then peered into the fog ahead of them. "Think the guy knows he's being trailed?"

"I knew it. I could tell almost from the first, by the way Cosmo worked, that she was being carried. I don't think the kidnapper knew of my tailing him until a few minutes ago. Otherwise he wouldn't have rested so much and let us get this close. But the chopper was a sure giveaway."

"It really didn't accomplish much since it couldn't set down through the fog, but they had hoped to contact you. We're way out of radio range of headquarters, especially in the hills and this fog. They took Tank out in an ambulance, and I came up in my pickup."

Often a tree came between them, and she passed on one side of it and he on the other.

"Tank says you should quit now. You should come in and let the state police and FBI handle it."

"And what am I—a potted plant?"

"Hey, don't get mad at me, okay? I'm just relaying the sheriff's message." He grinned. "I told him you didn't know the meaning of the word 'quit.' "

Their conversation was punctuated by the twisting and dodging required to miss the larger trees and by constantly pushing back the branches of the smaller ones. No Grimm Brothers forest could be denser.

"I told him that as long as Cosmo has the trail, I'm going on," Lucky said.

The trees pressed even closer and King dropped behind her in single file. She felt his presence on her back, but now she could cease to worry about the emotions he might read in her face. And perhaps, as the situation demanded, she could be an undistracted, professional police officer equal to the task.

"Okay, halt." King stopped and plucked at her coat sleeve. "I told him you'd never give up. So I brought provisions."

Lucky gasped. "Food?" She halted the bloodhound.

He grinned. "Food, water, and dog food." He glanced around them for a relatively open space and lowered his pack. "And coffee."

He passed her a thermos of coffee, and while she eagerly poured a cup, he emptied dry dog food from a sandwich bag onto a paper plate and set it before Cosmo. When the dog looked to Lucky for permission to eat, she said, "It's okay, boy, eat it."

As Cosmo leaned to the food, long ears trailing

in the plate, his droopy jowls snuffled like a vacuum cleaner.

Watching the ravenous dog gulp the food at her okay, King raised a questioning eyebrow.

"I've taught him not to take food from strangers," Lucky explained, wrapping her chilled hands around the coffee cup and blowing away its steam. "Helps protect him against poisoning."

He nodded. "Smart." He unpacked sandwiches, and while she ate, he refilled her canteen with water from a plastic jug.

Lucky gulped a sandwich, ever mindful of the time it was taking from Amy's trail. King watched her face while she ate. Overhead a few birds complained about the fog. Occasionally one flitted from branch to branch, but none risked flying very far in the poor visibility. As an excuse not to meet King's eyes, she pretended to watch them. Wrapped in the cottonlike fog, the forest was unnaturally quiet.

Presently King cut the bottom third from the jug and filled it with water from another canteen in his pack. He set the makeshift water dish in front of the bloodhound, who thanked him with a wave of his tail.

Lucky watched King's movements, and when he turned his back to her to pet the lapping dog, she studied the way his dark hair curled out from under his cap.

He glanced over his shoulder and caught her

staring. "I'm your backup," he said. "It might be another six hours before those guys down there get organized. They're moaning about the weather and terrain."

"From the way Cosmo's working, it'll be all over by then."

He stowed their trash into his pack. "Tank said he'll send a car back up Push Mountain Road to at least relay radio messages for us. As soon as he gets his shoulder seen to, he'll come himself."

In the meantime, Lucky realized, they were on their own. Back on the trail, she shoved away her awareness of King behind her and concentrated on the eager bloodhound tugging her through the misty forest. Only occasionally now did he drop his nose to the ground. Head up, taking the scent directly from the air, he heaved into his harness and lunged against the lead, his tail stiffly erect.

"Who called about the ransom?" she asked over her shoulder.

"Some woman. The authorities don't think the kidnapping was planned, but how he made the connection and arranged for the ransom call, they haven't yet figured out."

He followed Lucky so closely that it seemed he breathed nearly in her ear. She tried to avoid pushing aside branches for fear they would rebound in his face. "Did they consider the fact that he might have a portable radio?"

He ignored her question. "The little girl's family

hasn't got any money. He probably just found her wandering in the woods and seized the opportunity for a ransom. Maybe, at first, all he thought of was a reward."

She tried to penetrate the hazy veil ahead of them, and resisted Cosmo's demand for more speed. At this rate they could run onto the kidnapper before they spotted him.

"And the caller said that the guy threatened to harm the little girl if anybody came after him. The way I see it," King went on, "you're Amy's only hope. You and me. There's no time for anyone else."

"And Cosmo." She voiced a nagging fear: "King, what if he gets mean and hurts her if we get too close? I mean, shouldn't we maybe hang back a little and make him think some of the heat's off? I don't see how he could know about Cosmo."

"You're right," he said immediately. "Good idea. Besides, you look like you could use a rest."

She took a deep breath. "That's not important." Neither were the ticks, nor the chigger bites, nor the gouges of trees and brushy undergrowth, nor the fact that she probably looked like a fugitive cavewoman in the presence of the man she loved and hadn't seen for five years. "The only thing that matters is finding Amy, safe and sound." She half turned her head toward him. "I don't want to stop. I just want to slow down and give him some breathing room. I can't figure out where he's headed anyway. Tank mentioned the bluffs."

"Yeah, I know. On the other hand, if he gets too far ahead of us, he can make his way along the bluff until he finds a way down. He may even know of one that I don't." His tone of voice said he doubted it.

"Then we could just radio to have somebody pick him up on the river. Couldn't we?"

He grunted. "Maybe. If we can get a relay set up. But I have a feeling this guy has more than one hole to his burrow. And there's no question that he knows this forest like the palm of his hand. One thing for sure, though. If the fog lifts, the FBI and the state police will be swarming in here."

"And obliterating what's left of the trail." She studied the bloodhound. Despite the food and water, Cosmo panted heavily. Even in the cool damp air, his tongue dripped saliva. He needed rest badly.

She slowed her pace and resisted his tugs on the lead. "Okay. We'll cut him some slack, catch our breaths, and just stay with him."

In silence they threaded their way through the forest. Lucky tried to forget King's presence and concentrated on keeping the bloodhound's lead from tangling in the trees between them.

Unlike most of the trails she had followed with Cosmo, this one did not wander aimlessly. Sometimes the trail followed a ridgetop for some distance and afforded easier walking; sometimes it led obliquely down the side of a hill and rose sharply to climb the next, veering only when necessary to avoid a rocky outcropping or sheer drop-off. Wherever the kidnapper was going, he seemed to have a destination and was heading there as directly as possible.

Lucky pictured in her mind the map of the national forest and the Leatherwood Wilderness in particular. Sometime soon they should strike a large creek. If it had flooded since the kidnapper passed this way with the child, the scent might be nearly impossible to find on the other side. If, indeed, there was a way to cross.

But even before they descended into the hollow, she knew the creek was up but not out of its banks. It chased noisily down the mountain, advertising its presence long before it came into view through the fog. In contrast to the eerie silence of the fog-shrouded woods, the rushing water seemed very loud. At this lower altitude, they had dropped below the fog, which, impaled in the treetops, hung over them like a ceiling. As she picked her way down the steep pitch of the hillside, Lucky pushed away thoughts of how desperately she had so recently scrambled up a hill similar to this one.

But unlike the stream from which she and Tank had escaped, this one had carved a bluff of solid rock from the opposite hillside. The far bank below the bluff was only a narrow shelf of mud held in place by a few reedy plants, now winter-brown and brittle. Lucky shuddered. If the other creek had had such a bluff, escape would have been impossible. The flood waters, instead of spreading between two hills, would have been channeled down the narrow canyon at a much faster rate. She wondered how vulnerable they were to a sudden similar rise of this riverlike creek.

Hand over hand she hauled in the dog's lead and braced herself for a lunge. He would not hesitate to leap into the treacherous current to follow the trail of scent. But he lapped hungrily at the muddied stream while Lucky told herself that his need for water justified the risk.

King pointed out the footprints in the soft bank a few feet upstream, but said nothing. The chances of their belonging to anyone besides the kidnapper were extremely remote, especially given the weather conditions. He squatted and studied the footprints, memorizing the tread of the shoes that had made them.

Lucky remembered how often words had seemed unnecessary between them, then caught herself up short. First the work, then the daydreams.

When Cosmo had drunk all the water she thought was good for him, she gave the command to return to work. To her surprise, the bloodhound worked the trail downstream through the narrow gorge, away from the anticipated direction of the kidnapper. Perhaps he had decided that it would be too dangerous to attempt a crossing of the rain-swollen creek.

To King's puzzled look she replied, "Remember, he's trailing Amy, not the man. He must have set her down here."

King nodded and squinted into the fog downstream. Lucky knew without being told that he was worried about an ambush. Anyone crazy enough to kidnap a child would stop at nothing—not even murder.

Cosmo worked slowly along the bank, giving Lucky time to study the ground, in vain, for signs of Amy. Perhaps the swollen creek had washed her prints away.

After a few minutes of casting for the strongest scent of Amy in the soft ground along the creek, Cosmo bounded ahead downstream, sure of his direction. He lunged against the lead and towed Lucky after him. He thought they were close behind his quarry.

"You can get around this creek and its tributaries, but you have to go *up*stream for several miles," King shouted over the roar.

Lucky heard a note of puzzlement in his voice to match her own, but she did not question Cosmo's lead.

Behind a large boulder, Cosmo found the answer. A giant white oak, killed in the recent past by lightning, had been undermined by the creek. Losing its tenuous hold on the rocky bank, it had toppled across the stream to form a footbridge across the dangerously swift current.

More than three feet in circumference near the ground, the fifty-foot oak gradually narrowed as it crossed the creek. The first of its still-leafy branches, dried brown, rested just above the water on the other bank. She could not see the portion of treetop that was surely underwater, large limbs that could function either as anchors to help hold the trunk in place, or as rudders against which the current could push.

If the stream rose much higher, the huge log might be swung downstream and washed away from the far bank. There would be no other way across.

The bloodhound never faltered. He leaped onto the trunk and scrambled for a clawhold on the rough bark. When Lucky did not immediately follow, he lunged against the lead and whined. There was no doubt that Amy had crossed the makeshift bridge.

Lucky hesitated. She would eventually attempt to cross the creek on the tree trunk, she knew, but she preferred to first catch her breath and her equilibrium. She stood near the tangled mass of tree roots, bits of rocky soil still dangling from them, and watched the angry current roil inches beneath the trunk, tumbling and dragging under every branch and log that came down the creek, whisking them away at a vast speed.

King pounded up beside her and gave a low whistle. "Want me to go first?"

"No." As backup, he would be more valuable to her to wait behind and call for reinforcements if she didn't make it. "Wait until I'm clear across, please," she said, checking the waist harness. She squatted to inspect Cosmo's harness and the length of the lead linking them together. Muscles in her calves quivered and reminded her of the weariness settling on her like a suit of armor.

"I've got a rope in my pack," King said. "I never come into these mountains without one, but it isn't long enough for this job."

Lucky said nothing. Even rested and without the load on her back, she would fear the all-too-temporary log bridge. But she knew she had delayed long enough.

Waiting on the butt of the trunk, Cosmo whimpered impatiently.

"Will he cross it?" King asked, pitching his voice above the roar of the creek. "I know an old coonhound would, hot on a trail, but. . . ."

"He'll cross it." She took a deep breath. "The question is, will I?"

He reached for her right hand, held it in both of his, and then gently traced a long cut on her palm with a callused finger. "You'll cross it," he said.

Lucky lifted her head and gazed into his eyes for a long moment. She felt the five years between them vanish. She felt his warmth and strength flow into her.

He lifted her hand to his lips and kissed her fingertips. "You can do anything. Just take it slow and easy and remember to allow for the weight of the dog against your balance." He squeezed her hand and let it go. "Give me your backpack. I can manage both of them easier than you can manage one and the dog."

She started to protest, but he stopped her with a wave of his hand. "Don't be heroic. That's what I'm here for." He helped her shrug out of her pack, then backed away from the tree trunk.

She took a deep breath and wrenched her gaze from his. Wrapping the lead around her left hand to help minimize the chance of Cosmo's jerking her off balance, she clambered onto the trunk. Winding the strap around her hand a few more turns, she cinched the dog closer to her.

For a moment she fought the dizzying effect of the water rushing by beneath her feet. She countered by watching Cosmo's powerful haunches, which helped her to be prepared for his next move and how it might affect her balance.

Thus hampered in his movement, the bloodhound lifted his nose and followed the scent, mincing out onto the trunk over the water. Slowly and carefully, testing each foothold before committing his weight, he moved inexorably along the log.

Even in her terror Lucky admired the dog's intelligence and behavior. She swallowed and fought the urge to hold her breath. Depriving her brain of oxygen would hardly solve her immediate problems. She threw her free arm into space to help balance herself against Cosmo's movements.

A third of the way across, she became aware that sweat trickled down her sides, and she forced her mind back to total concentration. Cosmo hesitated unexpectedly and she bumped him with her knee. The dog scrambled for his balance while she watched helplessly. He resumed his progress with a jerk that threatened her own equilibrium.

Whitecaps on the surface of the water marked submerged rocks. Some of the underwater obstructions were large enough to cause the water to appear to boil and foam as it flowed over and around them. To be driven into a boulder by the force of the water would mean certain disaster. She wrenched her gaze back to the log.

It occurred to her that the bark on the trunk might have partially rotted in places, making it spongy or even loose underfoot. She tested her next step, but in so doing she destroyed the rhythm that had developed between her and the bloodhound along the short length of nylon strap linking them. He jerked against the lead and ran for a few steps to catch his balance. She had no choice but to follow, too quickly and precariously.

When Cosmo had recovered his balance, he halted and tested the air. Lowering his great head to the log, his nose worked against the bark. Then he tested the scent in the air.

Lucky tensed. Somehow, based on years of bloodhound experience, of observation and study, she knew in advance the dog's next move.

"Cosmo, no!" she shouted, and braced herself for his lunge.

Even as she yelled, the bloodhound gathered himself to leap into the water. At her command he hesitated and flung her a glance over his shoulder, his sad eyes puzzled.

"No, Cosmo," she repeated evenly. "I understand what you've told me," she said, trying to sound soothing even as she raised her voice above the roar of the rushing water. "Now just move on across the log, and we'll deal with it from there." She had no doubt that he understood from her tone what she expected of him. But even more compelling was that "find" command and his terrible need to follow the trail. "Go on, boy. That's right, go on across. It'll be all right."

In response to her low urging and the calm reassurance in her voice, with one more accusatory glance over his shoulder, the dog moved quickly and surely to the end of the log. Lucky followed onto the narrower end with the quick, little steps of a tightrope walker, and arrived at the end of the bridge in time to leap lightly to the muddy ground behind the bloodhound.

Almost before he had landed, Cosmo tried again

to enter the swollen creek. His paws scrambled in the mud without effect as Lucky leaned against his plunging.

"Sit and stay!" she commanded with all her authority.

Whimpering, Cosmo sat, and once more Lucky gave thanks for the months of obedience training through which they had both suffered.

No sooner had she cleared the log bridge than King leaped onto the trunk and edged out over the creek, Lucky's backpack dangling from a strap hooked over his left arm.

But at that moment the tree shuddered as its top, yielded to the force of the current, and rolled a couple of turns along the bank away from Lucky.

King rode the rolling log like a lumberjack, arms waving at his sides. But he had already lost his balance when the top of the tree slipped farther down the opposite bank and the trunk jerked downstream. Lucky stifled a scream as King fell into the icy water. Her backpack disappeared under the surface.

He threw his body upstream in the hope that it would lodge against the tree rather than be swept away from it. Because his arm was outstretched, he was able to grasp the trunk as he fell and prevent being pushed under it by the force of the water. Clinging desperately to the tree with one hand, he fought the powerful current to lift his head and upper body above the surface and to grip the trunk with his other arm. His cap disappeared under the surface and did not reappear. Buoyed by the water, his backpack rode high on his shoulders and hampered the movements of his arms.

Once both hands had found the log, he battled the torrent to lift the rest of his body out of the creek. While the current worked to drag him under the trunk, he hauled himself up with the strength of his upper body. Coughing and gagging, he sprawled face down on the trunk.

Lucky realized she had been holding her breath, and shuddered. She was about to cry out when King scrambled to his feet, got his balance on the trunk, and made short work of the crossing.

To hide her stricken face from his view, she concentrated on unwinding the lead from her palm and rechecking the harness. When he stood at her side, she took his arm with a trembling hand and hoped that her concern for his safety showed in her eyes. But he still faced the very real danger of hypothermia. She longed to cling to him, to hold him, and to be held by him. But Amy Roberts, if she was still alive, needed her.

Still breathless, King acknowledged her feelings with a smile and gripped her hand.

"What's up?" he asked. Dripping muddy water, he clenched his jaws to keep his teeth from chattering. "What's the matter with Cosmo?"

Lucky pointed a shaking finger. "Amy went into the water there."

He jerked as though she had struck him. "What? Did he drop her? Throw her?" He rubbed his arms vigorously as he spoke.

"I don't know." Dumbstruck with horror at Amy's possible fate and King's close call, she stared into the muddy torrent. "All I know is, Cosmo said she went in." She held King's eyes. "She went in probably not long ago. I've got to go on. You'd better build a fire and dry out before you freeze to death." Without waiting for his response, she whirled to the dog. "Cosmo, find."

Rested by the slight delay, the bloodhound leaped into action. As if understanding that his mistress would not allow him to follow the scent into the water, he concentrated on finding traces of it downstream. Herded by the sheer bluff dangerously near the edge of the swollen creek, he sought the stronger scent that would indicate Amy's emergence from the water.

King shouted after her. "I have a change in my pack. I'll catch up." His voice echoed in the narrow canyon.

Thinking she should have known that King would be prepared for almost anything, Lucky waved a hand in acknowledgment but did not look back. A waterproof pack, clothes rolled in a slicker—no doubt he had even included a shelter tent and more food.

She ran after Cosmo, no longer working to slow the dog down. Speed might be everything now. She shoved King's plight out of her thoughts and concentrated on keeping her feet in the greasy mud and searching the ground for traces of Amy.

But though she tried to divorce her emotions from the job at hand, her gaze kept sweeping downstream, half expecting to see a child's body bobbing in the unforgiving current or lodged in a pile of debris.

Chapter Eight

*A*fter racing straight away for perhaps fifty yards, the creek veered sharply back to the south, impeded by a tower of rock that had sheared away from the cliff. But behind the tower, a quieter pool had formed where the stream chiseled and sucked at the base of the bluff. Water swirled into the pool and eddied against the bank. A dam of driftwood and other flotsam, including her own backpack, proved that a current moved into the space behind the tower.

Cosmo hesitated for a heartbeat over footprints in the muddy shore. Lucky recognized the tread in the prints, still filling with water. A very short time ago at this spot, the kidnapper had pulled Amy from the creek.

The child must still be alive, Lucky concluded. The man would surely not have retrieved her body. But at best she was soaking wet and dangerously chilled, had swallowed flood water, and was probably injured in the rocky torrent. The danger posed by the kidnapper was now compounded by the threat of exposure, hypothermia, and shock.

Behind the tower the bluff ended. The bloodhound whirled and plunged into the deep forest crowding the bank. Though it could be climbed, the hill out of the hollow was almost a cliff. Slowly, tortuously, Cosmo scrambled upward into the fog, hauling Lucky after him. The trail here was more than Amy's scent. Broken limbs, skid marks in the muddy soil, disturbed rocks—there was no question that they were headed correctly and that the kidnapper knew he was being pursued.

They topped the crest of the hill at last, only to plunge immediately into the next hollow. Lucky remembered from the topographical map that one east-west ridge after another rolled away into the distance. Heading north meant plunging down one nearly perpendicular hill, slipping and sliding, half sitting at times, and arduously climbing the next. She hauled herself up by grasping tree trunks and vines. Unlike larger rocks that could be stepped on or over, small stones rolled underfoot, making it painfully easy to wrench a knee or turn an ankle.

She became dimly aware of King a few steps behind her, but she pushed all thoughts of him from her mind. Once Amy was safe, there would be time for King.

The mist increased to a steady drizzle, and at times the fog was so thick she could scarcely see the huge dog twenty feet ahead of her. She longed for an end to this stretch of hilly terrain. But when it came, the terrain was even more rugged. Their quarry led them onto a high plain of solid rock like a horizontal bluff. Perhaps he mistakenly thought that scent would be difficult or impossible to detect here.

When the bloodhound began to limp, Lucky knew without examining his feet that the pads were cut and bruised. Even the thick soles of her own heavy hiking shoes were inadequate protection from the punishing rocks. She had no way of determining time or distance since crossing the swollen creek, but guessed they had struggled northward after Amy and her kidnapper for almost three hours at two miles an hour.

She welcomed the resumption on the plateau of the dense forest with its cushion of pine needles and wet leaves. But gradually the trees began to yield to occasional openings, and a Forest Service sign announced the end of the official wilderness. Once more they were within the national-forest boundary. The clearings were man-made, old fields once wrestled from the woods and then abandoned when the poor, thin soil was quickly exhausted.

In the thick fog it was like moving in a bubble. Beyond a few feet the fog shut out the rest of the universe, but always Cosmo led on eagerly, straining at the lead and urging her to more speed, sure sign of a fresh trail.

Lucky wondered at the hound's sense of urgency. What compelled him to run rather than take the easier way of a leisurely walk? Did he sense her own desperation? Or was he aware, on some level, of the importance of his mission?

Finally they stumbled onto an old dirt road. Mature trees crowded its very edge, their branches intertwining overhead. In the lushness of summer, the road would be a shady tunnel. Already, fresh spring grass edged the muddy track, and a slender ribbon of green down its middle indicated that the road still saw occasional traffic—maybe of backwoods hunters of mushrooms and ginseng, wild turkeys and deer. Though the forest struggled to heal the scar, the narrow opening between the trees made for easier trailing. Still limping, Cosmo picked up the pace, confident of the scent.

King jogged up beside her and asked, "How are you doin'?" His resourceful backpack had yielded a knit cap to replace the one lost to the flooded stream, and damp hair curled around his forehead under it.

She gave him a smile and hoped her fatigue was not blatantly obvious. "Okay. I think we're very close behind them."

Suddenly the bloodhound swerved off the road and paused at the overgrown lane to an abandoned homesite. Head high, sniffing the air, he stalked toward a clearing heavily overgrown with tall weeds and young homesteading trees.

With her left hand Lucky gathered in the lead

and shortened Cosmo's distance from her. This might be the end of the trail. A native stone well house, door ajar, stood under a giant oak. In its darkened interior might lurk any number of dangers, human or otherwise. Behind it, an old outhouse loomed out of the fog and the waist-high weeds.

The only trace of the dwelling was a corner of foundation, some rotted shoes nearly buried in damp leaves, and a dirt-encrusted perfume bottle, still a startling blue against the mist. Near the apparent corner of the former front porch stood a dogwood tree, its first blossoms a glowing white in the gloom.

King took her arm and said, "Wait. Let me go in first." Squinting into the fog, he started ahead.

Lucky grasped his sleeve. "No, King, don't confuse the scent. Just stay close on my left." With her right hand she unsnapped her holster, withdrew her handgun, and flipped off the safety. She allowed Cosmo a little slack on the lead, and the dog pulled hard into the ghost-filled yard.

Then, as though checked by an invisible hand, Cosmo stopped short. The loose skin of his wrinkled brow slid forward as he nosed the ground.

Lucky's gaze swept the clearing and saw nothing that was visible in the fog. Keeping her gun level, she leaned to inspect Cosmo's find. His tail stiffly outstretched, the hair standing up along his spine, he nuzzled an assortment of bones, a canine skeleton, judging by the teeth still set in the jawbone, crushing molars and enormous fangs.

King let out his breath. "So that's it."

Lucky shook her head. "I don't think so. He's trained to ignore distractions." She studied the outbuildings again for a sign of their quarry. "Maybe Amy handled this, or kicked at it." Some of the bones had been disturbed, a few scattered to one side of the main skeleton. "I think it's likely that she's in one of these buildings, alone or otherwise."

King peered into the fog. "Then let's have a look."

Cosmo left the skeleton and plunged toward the rear of the clearing. Lucky strained to see ahead of them. Just before Cosmo reentered the woods, he veered to the right. Behind a stand of young oaks as high as her head, Lucky caught a glimpse of a large hole scooped out of the hillside.

"Looks like an old storm cellar," King said. "Careful. It's a good hiding place."

Lucky cocked the revolver and gripped the dog's lead tightly to keep him from pulling her off balance. Slowly she advanced. The earthen hollow held only trash and household refuse. "Nothing," she said as she lowered the revolver. "False alarm." All she had accomplished was spangling her uniform and coat with beggar's-lice to accompany her other battle scars. But Cosmo still strained to advance to the edge of the clearing.

Then, through the unnatural quiet of the fog,

Lucky heard the hoarse sobbing of a child. She whirled to King, but before they could react, a man broke from behind a huge walnut tree at the far edge of the clearing and crashed into the woods. In his arms struggled a little girl, her light hair and pale face stark against the man's dark form. Her angry screams filled the forest while tiny fists beat at her kidnapper's shoulder.

Lucky planted her feet solidly and leveled the revolver even though she knew she couldn't fire for fear of hitting Amy. "Halt!" she shouted.

The man never broke his stride. He shifted Amy under one arm and held her close to his body to discourage Lucky's bullet. Though bulky and long-legged, he moved effortlessly between the trees without a backward glance. With the grace of long custom he leaped a fallen log in his path and dodged a giant walnut. Lucky caught a glimpse of denim overalls topped by a quilted black jacket. Grasping limbs slid easily off its nylon shell. A matching cap was pulled so low over his brow that Lucky could see little of his face other than a rusty beard streaked with gray.

She jammed the revolver into its holster and released her hold on Cosmo's lead. Soundlessly the dog bounded into the woods after Amy. Tail erect, head up, the scent unimpeded by the vagaries of wind or the erosion of time, he leaned into the harness and plunged with every step, sore paws forgotten or ignored.

Running behind the pull of the eager blood-hound, Lucky tried to focus on the child. Her cries had ceased, and she appeared to jounce limply under the kidnapper's arm. Lucky glanced over her shoulder at King.

"Go for it!" he shouted. "I'm right behind you."

Leaping boulders in her path, Lucky burst out of the trees, glad for the easier going of the old road. Their quarry had disappeared into the fog.

She watched the hound, studying his movements, anticipating his direction, and managing the lead to keep it from snagging on brushy new growth.

In the sameness of the foggy forest and her own jarring run, Lucky lost track of direction and of time. She could see nothing beyond the next couple of steps. But it didn't matter. Wherever Cosmo led, she would follow. He had trailed Amy's scent through some of the roughest country in the world. He had earned her complete faith and trust. Again she vowed never again to begrudge any time spent in training, either her own body or the dog.

She concentrated on coordinating her breathing with her footfalls, on filling her lungs and keeping her blood and brain oxygenated. Wherever possible she gripped the nylon strap with a hand to help protect her balance from the shocks of the plunging bloodhound on the other end.

King's footfalls were no longer audible over the pounding of her own heart in her ears. If he had fallen behind or even been forced to a halt, it did not matter. Nothing mattered but little Amy, who had been through so much and now hung unconscious, as limp as a rag doll, from her kidnapper's arms.

But then an awareness of change intruded, a feeling of height, an overwhelming sensation of nothingness ahead. The forest and its thick vegetation continued unchanged, but even as she strained to see through the fog and drizzle, she sensed the truth.

The bluff. The five hundred-foot drop that Tank had warned her of so many miles ago—the sheer rock face of the White River, the northern boundary of the Ozark National Forest. Twenty-five feet from the edge, she could have stopped herself, would have been aware of the danger in time. But single-minded Cosmo, following the trail of the lost child and aware of nothing else, did not stop.

She hauled back on the lead with both hands, dug in with her heels, and screamed a command. It was too late. The bloodhound charged over the edge of the cliff and sailed into the abyss. Scrambling desperately to hold him and catch herself, Lucky clawed the air in vain for something to cling to.

Leashed inexorably to him by the harness around her waist, she flew into space behind the dog. She landed once, hard, a glancing blow, then bounced again into the void.

She screamed, or meant to, but as in a nightmare, no sound escaped her. Her first thought was of Amy. Could King find her without the bloodhound? Would he be aware of the bluff in time?

With a jolt that racked her with pain and knocked the air from her lungs, her body stopped short far sooner than she'd expected. She gasped for air and fought the haze of unconsciousness. After a moment she became aware of the rain on her face.

Opening her eyes to disorientation, to the sight of nothing except the fog, she turned her head. Fighting a dizzying terror, she realized that somehow she had caught on to something on the way down; she hung face up from the side of the bluff. When she twisted slightly to look for Cosmo, her body swung free and vertigo threatened to overwhelm her.

Grasping the air for something to hold on to, she fought for control of her wits and her emotions. Though she could not see him, she sensed that Cosmo hung a few feet below her. Even as she realized his location, the dog began to struggle wildly. As he did, her own body jangled in the air.

"*Stay,* Cosmo," she squeaked in an effort to speak calmly and soothingly to the terrified dog. She fought the hysteria rising in her throat and prayed he did not sense her fear. Apparently the twenty-foot strap linking them together had snagged on something, a tree perhaps. But how far they were from the top of the bluff, or from almost certain death on the rocky bottom of the shallow river below, she did not know.

The bloodhound wriggled violently in an effort to touch his feet to something solid. The wet lead slipped in his direction and Lucky slammed against the bluff.

She fought waves of pain and horror. "Easy, boy," she crooned. "It's okay. Take it easy."

"*Lucky?*" King's voice overhead sounded incredulous but terror-stricken.

"Help us! We're caught on something. The lead is caught, dangling. . . ." Hysteria bubbled up and she broke off. Though she could not see King above her in the fog, the relative brightness straight ahead and the pain in her back convinced her she was hanging face up.

"Hang on!" he shouted. "Just hang on. I'll get my rope."

Her teeth began to chatter and she clenched her jaws tightly. "Easy, boy, easy . . ." she said to Cosmo.

The dog jerked and crashed into the bluff, sending a shock wave along the lead that propelled her farther into space. She choked on a scream and drew in her arms and legs to prepare herself for the crash as her body came slamming back against the stone.

Dislodged by the impact, bits of rock broke away from the cliff and, long moments later, splashed into the river below. She fumbled blindly for a handhold, her bare fingers rasping over the stone. Then they closed over a slender twig and she clung to it, desperate to halt her pendulous swings caused by the struggling dog on the other end of the lead.

"Lucky?" King's voice overhead was thin and strained. "Rope coming down," he said even as the end of a rope dangled tantalizingly a few feet from her head.

She grabbed for the rope, her movements causing her body to swing in space. Frantically she wound the end of the rope around her left hand. Disturbed by her motion, Cosmo thrashed in the air. She felt the lead slip again and caught her breath.

"Listen to me," King ordered.

She longed to be able to see him standing above her, and strained to understand him through her terror.

"I've worked my way out onto a sloping ledge to reach you. I have the rope hitched around a tree up here. I think it's dead and don't know how strong it is." His voice was tight with effort. "I'm going to pull you up a little at a time, keeping the rope taut. Do you understand?"

"Yes," she cried, picturing him leaning into space, endangering his own life to save hers.

"Tie the rope to that belt around your waist," King ordered.

"I can't. Every time I move, the lead slips down toward Cosmo. I think it's snagged."

Overhead King's boots scraped on stone, and then a shower of rocks rebounded into the chasm. The sound of their falling echoed into the distance. "Listen, I can just barely see you," King said. "The lead is caught on a dead tree sticking out from the side of the bluff. It's pretty well around the butt of the tree and seems secure for the moment. But I don't know how strong the tree is with both of your weights on it. You aren't far down, maybe twenty feet below me, but you're hanging under a projection of rock like a chin, and that's going to make it tough." Like the falling stones, his voice echoed in the abyss.

Another rain of stones told Lucky that King had edged farther down the slope toward them. "Loop the rope through the waist harness and tie it securely," he ordered. "I wish we had enough to go around you under your arms too, but we don't." He paused, and Lucky imagined him studying her predicament. "Once you're out from under the overhang, you should be able to sort of walk your way up the face of the cliff with the rope to hang on to. It's the only way. Tie on the rope now."

Moving slowly and carefully, Lucky obeyed. Her slightest movement causing her to swing into space, she forced her concentration onto the tying of the knot. Unable to raise her head high enough to see her hands without swinging farther over the abyss and then crashing into the bluff, she maneuvered the rope into the knot by feel, full of belated gratitude to a father who had insisted that his little girl learn to tie knots.

Meanwhile King talked to the bloodhound, his voice soft and soothing. Cosmo hung limp, his whimpers echoing around them.

When the rope was securely knotted through her waist harness, Lucky took a deep breath. "I'm ready," she called, her voice quavering only slightly. She squinted into the fog in the hope of catching a glimpse of King overhead, but gaps in the fog permitted her a view of only the overhanging rock. Like a roof over her head, it protruded from the face of the main bluff for perhaps ten feet.

"Okay now, listen," King ordered, his voice strong and confident. "This is going to be a little tricky because of Cosmo. When I start to pull you up and your weight lifts off his lead and that tree, he's going to be dangling from your waist harness. Since I doubt you're willing to cut him loose, you've got to get into a position to pull him in close to you before you start up. That's going to be tough. Understand?"

"Tell me what to do. I'm ready," she said. Cosmo deserved nothing less than her total commitment. He would be saved with her or they would die together.

Echoing out of the fog, King's voice sounded otherworldly: "Okay, first you've got to brace your

feet against the bluff. Grab hold of the rope above
you, pull yourself upright, and swing around until
you can put your feet out in front of you and brace
them on the bluff. Understand?"

"Yes," she replied.

"Now remember—the dog's weight is going to
hit you sooner or later. Use one hand on the rope
and one on the lead as soon as you can, or he'll
break you in two."

"Here goes."

"And be prepared for him to struggle."

She gripped the rope with both hands and
thought longingly of her deerskin gloves lost in the
flood. Without her coat, her arms would have been
shredded raw by now. By pulling on the rope, she
maneuvered herself into an upright position and
hung from the rope instead of the lead. She twisted
her body to face the cliff and kicked up her feet.
They slid on the wet stone and the movement propelled her away from the bluff. She felt Cosmo's
weight on the waist harness and glanced down.

She could see him now, no longer wriggling, but
twisting at the end of the lead like a spent yo-yo.
His whimpers echoed in the canyon. Giving her full
attention to the bluff, she saw an area of rougher
stone where her soles might find traction. "I'm
gonna swing to my left a little," she called to King.

"Roger," he shouted. "Remember to allow for
Cosmo's weight on the lead."

Feeling stronger, and confident of King's help

with the lifeline, she pushed off the bluff with one foot and swung her body to the left. Flexing her knees to absorb the impact, she extended her legs toward the patch of roughened stone. She bounced twice, but the soles of her boots could cling to the face of the cliff. The lead followed her over the tree holding Cosmo, and though the tree still bore most of the burden, she felt his dead weight around her waist.

"I'm going to haul Cosmo in now," she said. Letting go of the rope with her right hand, she wrapped it around her left palm to ensure her grip. Then she grasped the lead and began to haul Cosmo closer to her. Because his weight on the other end of the line allowed no slack, she had no choice but to wrap the lead around her palm as she inched him toward her.

When the bloodhound hung even with the tree that had broken their fall, he was still out of her reach. The lead snagged on a branch of the tree and defied her efforts to free it. It occurred to her that if the lead came loose, the dog's weight would be all on her waist. She had no choice but to rappel back to the tree, untangle the lead, and hold on to Cosmo's harness.

She pushed away from the cliff with her feet, and then threw her body sideways to the right toward the tree holding Cosmo. As she did so, loosening the tension on the short length of lead between them, the lead was released from the tree and all the dog's weight was transferred to the harness around her waist and the rope fastened to it.

Her rappeling maneuver went out of control, and she slammed into the bluff near the bloodhound. Without hesitation she grabbed for the spinning dog and grasped his harness at the shoulder. "Easy, boy," she gasped in an effort to calm him and quiet his piteous cries.

Pulling hard on the taut lifeline with her left hand, she clambered to get her feet once more on the face of the bluff. Scrambling to get a grip on the wet stone, she straightened into position for rappeling up the face of the bluff. She had no choice but to drag Cosmo after her, as rough on him as that might be.

"King! We're ready!"

"You can't come straight up because of the overhang I told you about. You'll have to rappel to your left as far as the rope will reach. Then, as I haul on the line, just walk your way up the bluff. I'll take up the slack as you come."

The lifeline lurched as King started to haul them up. She pictured him straining into the rope he had hitched around the tree above them, the tree that now bore their combined weight and upon which their lives depended.

Still in the horizontal rappeling position, she swung to the left in three giant steps, hauling Cosmo behind her.

"That's good," King shouted. "Now come up."

Pulling herself up by the hand entwined in the lifeline, she walked up the face of the cliff as King took up the slack in the rope. Cosmo stared into the chasm, his long ears swinging. To calm his terror and quiet his struggles, she spoke softly to him as they inched upward: "We're gonna make it, fella. We're gonna be all right now."

She had almost come to believe it herself when she stopped to catch her breath. She looked up, and peering into the fog around them, hoped to catch a glimpse of King. But her gaze fell on the rope, their tenuous lifeline to the top of the bluff. Repeatedly sawed across the edge of the rocky projection that King had warned her about, the rope was as frayed and worn as if it had been chewed by rats.

"King, the rope . . . it's about to break!"

His reply sounded very close above her: "You can make it, Lucky. Come on. Straight up now, just like at police academy." He hauled on the rope, and it tugged at her left arm. Her right arm quivered with the strain of holding the writhing hound close to her side. Her feet were like chunks of lead.

"Come on, Lucky! You can do it. Just a little more now, just a little way to go. Come on." King's voice pulled at her like the rope. "Come on. Do it for Cosmo. Do it for me," he shouted, his voice echoing through the gorge. "Do it for me, Lucky, because I love you."

Love you . . . love you. . . . The echoes resounded over the river.

With a deep breath, Lucky shoved away her fatigue. A second chance . . . she'd been given a second chance for life. And a second chance to deserve King's love. She pulled hard on the lifeline and moved one foot and then the other up the face of the bluff.

King hauled in the slack and urged her on. "Come on now, just a few more feet." He pulled on the rope, hand over hand, drawing her up.

She moved her feet to help him, to reduce the amount of dead weight he would have to tug over the side of the cliff. Cosmo whined and clawed for a foothold on the bluff. But suddenly he seemed more interested in something below him than in reaching the top.

Lucky followed his gaze and looked down. Through the swirling fog she glimpsed a small figure on a mound of soil that had washed over the edge of the bluff and piled up, over the millenia, on a ledge some twenty-five feet below the rim and about five feet below her own stopping place. "Oh, no! It's Amy!" she cried.

Amy . . . Amy! the echo shouted, but the child did not look up. Her blond hair kinky with damp curls, Amy sprawled unconscious—or dead— beside a stunted cedar tree. If she moved an inch in any direction, it would mean disaster.

Chapter Nine

*L*ucky checked her emotional response. Now she must fall back on her training as a police officer and be dispassionate and controlled. Clearly, there was only one possible course of action—she must go back down the bluff after the little girl. But first she must unburden herself of Cosmo. A burst of adrenaline renewed her strength, and she gripped the lifeline and pulled harder to reach the top.

King gasped an oath when she told him about Amy. "Did he put her there or . . . ? She must have fallen over and he just left her there rather than risk a rescue. He knew we were right on his heels. He figured we'd go after her rather than stay on his trail."

"And I played right into his hands by going over myself," Lucky said breathlessly. She cursed herself for not realizing from the moment Cosmo ran over the cliff that he had merely done as he was bidden; he had followed Amy's trail. Amy had gone over the edge of the bluff ahead of them.

At last King's arms reached to gather her in from the void. His strong hand replaced hers on the bloodhound's harness. She collapsed against him on the stony ledge. Cosmo pushed against her legs.

"Come on, keep moving just a little longer," his voice urged in her ear. "We'd better get off this slope. It's not very stable."

She shook her head. "I've got to go back after Amy. If she comes to and moves around, she may fall to her death."

"First you've got to catch your breath and rest. You'll kill both yourself and her if you don't." With one arm around her and the other hand on Cosmo's harness, he led them to the top of the bluff and safety.

Lucky sat down and drew a quavering breath. King knelt beside her and took her in his arms. She leaned against him to stop her trembling, and felt that his body shook too. For what seemed a long time, he held her. And slowly the terror passed.

She lifted her head from his shoulder. "Oh, King, why did I ever think I could do this kind of work?" she asked. "I nearly got us killed." With a shudder she saw that the narrow dirt road stopped some fifty feet from the rim of the bluff. But the forest pressed on to its very edge. The ground simply fell away without warning.

He smoothed her wet hair and she realized for the first time that she had lost her cap to the river.

"In this fog, that could just as easily have been me if I'd been in the lead," he said, his voice low and soothing. "I blame myself for not reminding you of the bluff, for not keeping right on your heels." He held her tightly. "You're terrific, you know. You didn't panic and you did everything just perfect. Even male cops get in tight places and have to have help. That's why they have backups."

Cosmo rose and shook himself hard, as though he had just emerged from the river itself. When she pulled him to her side in a hug, he licked her hand and seemed to grin.

Then he turned and sniffed the air. Without hesitation he loped to the edge of the bluff, gathered his haunches, and prepared to leap again into the chasm.

She grabbed for the lead, hauled hard with both hands, and dug in with her heels. King reached across her and added his strength to stopping the bloodhound from throwing himself once more into the gorge. Cosmo tugged on the taut lead and whimpered. He lowered himself to the ground and hung his head over the rim of the cliff, his long ears drooping into the void.

"He's right," Lucky said. "I must go back down after Amy."

Even as she spoke, Lucky heard the child's cry. "Mommy, Mommy. . . ." Echoing eerily in the river gorge, Amy's wails filled the air, echoing and reechoing along the river.

Keeping Cosmo's lead taut, Lucky scrambled to her feet. Even as she formulated a plan, Cosmo belly-crawled at the end of his lead, inching his way along the rim of the cliff. His tail wagged happily; the lost was found.

"You want to move that rope for me?" she tossed over her shoulder as she checked the knot on the waist harness. Without waiting for an answer, she tugged Cosmo away from the brink, unhooked his lead from her harness, and fastened it around a nearby tree. The dog whined his disapproval. "Good dog, Cosmo!" More praise would have to wait.

"I'll go," King said. He sidled onto the rocky lip to retrieve the other end of the rope. "You've been through enough," he called up to her as he untied the knot.

She sought his eyes. "Not nearly as much as that little girl," she said. "Nobody else can get to her. Not the chopper, not—"

"*I* can!"

"Thanks, but you're physically stronger than me and I need you on the rope. And I'd rather trust myself to you than trust you to myself. Besides, I'm pretty well acquainted with the face of that cliff." She knelt on the edge of the bluff. "Amy?" she called. Her voice echoed over the river.

The child's cries ceased.

"Amy, listen to me." Lucky concentrated on calming her tone, on communicating reassurance to the terrified child. "My name is Lucky and I'm coming to get you." She waited for the echoes to subside before continuing. "Sit real still and wait for me right there, okay?"

Soft whimpers from the child were the only answer. Lucky was aware of King moving behind her, carefully tying the lifeline to the sturdy tree closest to her position.

"Amy, can you see me?" she called.

"No!" the child wailed. "I'm scared!" She sounded small and totally alone.

"I know right where you are," Lucky called. "I'll be there very soon. Just sit real still, okay?"

"My head hurts," Amy cried. "I want my mommy."

"I know, darling, but be sure to sit real still till I get there." Lucky got to her feet and, despite the continuing drizzle, shrugged out of her coat. "This thing was in the way before. How long before dark?"

King checked his watch. "Long enough, I hope." He caught her hand. "Listen, Lucky, this is very poor procedure."

"This whole operation is poor procedure, a mess from the beginning. If you have any better ideas, I'm open for suggestions."

He watched her hurried preparations in silence for a moment, then retrieved his backpack from where he had slung it upon discovering her plight. He knelt before it. "The thing is, the fog will get worse as it gets dark." He pulled a black sweater from his pack. "Here," he said, extending it to her. "You need something on your arms. And you'd better wear these." He snatched off his leather gloves.

Lucky shook her head. "You might need them more than I do." If she fell, he would be forced to haul her up on the rope, hand over hand.

Wordlessly he pocketed the gloves, then pulled the hunter-orange watch cap from his head. "At least take this." He got to his feet and crossed to her side. He ignored her pointed look at his own damp hair. "It'll help me see you in the fog."

He lifted the cap and, settling it gently on her wet head, tugged it tenderly into place over her ears.

She met his eyes and smiled into them. "Thank you," she whispered.

He stepped back, but his eyes never left her face as she coiled the rope between herself and the anchoring tree. Mostly to cover her reaction to his attention, Lucky studied the rope. "This poor, mistreated rope. I just hope it can hold up under another trip down there."

King grunted. "I admire you." When she looked up in surprise, he held her gaze for a long moment. "I mean, I love you, and I like you, but I also really do *admire* you."

Lucky leaned against him and kissed him on the

cheek. "Hold the thought," she whispered. "When this is over. . . ."

He cleared his throat. "I think the rope will be okay. I'm just worried that there's not enough of it."

She nodded. "Me too." She shrugged into his sweater. "But there's a place to the right of where I came up that's really just a very steep slope, a sort of slantwise shelf across the bluff for a little way before it drops off straight down." Breathlessly she hurried the words so that the explanation would cost her no time from Amy, whose echoing sobs filled the air. "There's a lot of loose rock washed in there, and some small cedars and scrubs, but I think I can make my way down and get her." She pushed up her sleeves and adjusted the sweater over the waist harness and the rope. "That ghoul might even have gone down there on purpose to throw us off."

"And then got away when you fell," King added grimly. "You're probably right. And desperate to just get away, he left Amy for us to find."

"But maybe not." She lifted the rope behind her and gave it a hard snap to test the knot at the tree. "Okay, I'm off. I can make it down okay without you. Why don't you try to raise Tank or someone at headquarters and have them send in a doctor or a medic to check her out before they take her in."

"Unless he's managed to get within two or three miles of us in the car, which I doubt, there's not much hope. What we've got here is a radio dead spot. Even if they heard us, they still can't fly in this soup. I think it's safe to say we're still pretty much on our own."

Amy's thin cry echoed in the gorge. "Help me, Lucky!"

"Okay, I'll be right there." Lucky turned back to King. "Then I guess you'll have to take her out, because I'll be going after that creep." She turned away from him and strode toward the edge of the bluff.

"Lucky. . . ."

She waved over her shoulder. "See if you can raise anybody on the radio, will you?"

She paid out the damp rope behind her and pulled it taut as she turned and backed over the rim of the cliff. The sheer face of the bluff rose on her right and she stayed as near to it as she could, away from the edge of the shelf. Loose stones rolled under her feet, and she fell to her knees on the steep pitch of the slope. She had gone only a few feet and already the rope had saved her from crashing over the bluff into the gorge. So much for her bravado. She glanced up and saw King's anxious face in the mist above her. "Piece of cake," she called.

He grunted. "Take it easy, will you?"

She looked down but could not yet see the child through the fog. "Here I come, Amy. Sit real still so I can find you," she called.

A current of air swirled the fog and at last she

could see Amy. Still below her and considerably to the right, the child was in a position that was even more tenuous than Lucky had realized. Little more than rocky mud, the hillock that had broken Amy's fall sluiced away in the rainfall even as Lucky watched. The gnarled cedar beside the child clung desperately to the face of the bluff by newly exposed roots. Her own position would be just as precarious if it were not for King and his rope. The meager soil on the slope was loose and, even where it had soaked up the rain, it was so rocky that it broke apart under her step and cascaded down the face of the bluff.

"I see you now," Amy cried. "Help me!" Her eyes were very dark and very large in a face white with fear. Short, damp hair curled in ringlets over her wide forehead. Her clothing seemed outsized but sparse, and her teeth chattered.

"I see you too, honey," Lucky called. "Remember now, hold very still."

Instead, Amy stood up. She caught her foot in the tail of her flowing garment and lost her balance. As she staggered to catch herself from falling, much of the soil on her slender perch broke away and plummeted into the abyss, leaving the child nothing beneath her feet. She grabbed for the cedar and clung to its tough branches against the side of the cliff. Her terrified whimpers seemed everywhere in the gorge.

"Hang on tight," Lucky said, keeping her voice

low and calm. "You'll be all right as long as you hold on to that tree. Understand me?"

"Help me!" Amy cried.

"I'm coming. Just hold on tight. I'll be there very soon." Lucky forced herself to test each step and proceed with caution. If she fell—or the rope broke—she would be of no help to the child.

As she descended, the branches of the scrubby trees on the slope clawed at her and she forced her way through them. In an effort to improve her vision, she wiped her face on the sleeve of King's sweater. In the hope of a better grip on the rope, she attempted to dry her hands. She bit her lip at the pain. Chapped as they were, cut by snags, scraped on the rocks, rope burned, her hands could not fail her now.

She lowered herself backward down the sloping face of the bluff, much too steep now to stand upright without the anchoring lifeline. With a glance to her right, she saw that she was at Amy's level at last. But still too far away from the child to reach her.

"Hurry, hurry!" Amy cried.

The child's sobs filled Lucky's head, and she struggled to clear her mind of fear and emotion, and to proceed cautiously and methodically as she had been trained. Hoping for more slack, she gave a tug on the rope.

"That's it," King yelled.

"Hold on tight, sweetie," Lucky called to Amy.

"I'll be there in a jiffy." She studied the face of the cliff separating her from the youngster. A narrow ledge ran across the face of the bluff between them, just wide enough for tiptoes. But since she was not a practiced rock climber, there was no way she could leave the safety of the rope and maneuver to Amy and then back to her own ledge, especially with a terrified child on her back for the return trip.

Nor was it feasible to retrace her steps, return to the top of the bluff, then rappel down the sheer face directly above Amy to her level. That would require precious moments they did not have, and still with no guarantee that the length of the rope would be sufficient. Not only was she out of rope, she was out of time too. Amy could not hold on to the sharp cedar much longer. Her cries of terror echoed in the canyon.

"King, I've got to have more rope!" She leaned her head back to peer into the fog, but could not see him above her.

"Just a minute," he replied, his voice sounding deceptively close in the fog. "I'm rigging something here with Cosmo's lead. Got something to hang on to for a second?"

She grasped a nearby cedar and molded herself to the cliff. "Okay," she called, and felt the rope at her waist go slack. Now, like Amy, only a shallow-rooted cedar kept her from the long fall to the rocks below. Hanging upside down beside her on the face of the bluff was the skeleton of a cedar that had lost its tenuous hold on the meager soil.

After the longest short interval she had ever known, she felt the rope tighten and grow taut again across her chest.

"Now listen."

She pictured King kneeling to lean over the edge of the bluff with his instructions.

"I've got you a few more feet."

"Great." She began to plan her approach to Amy.

"Wait a minute," he yelled. "I've tied Cosmo's lead onto the end of the rope. But it isn't safe and it'll be tricky taking up the slack. And I'm not sure the knot will hold."

"I don't plan on testing it."

Once again she turned her attention to the narrow ledge between them. It would be absurdly risky under the best of conditions. Now it was wet and slippery, but it was the only way.

"I'm going across a ledge to Amy," she called into the fog. "Be prepared for anything."

Finding a handhold to her right, Lucky edged onto the ledge with the toes of her right foot, then another handhold and the left foot. The taut lifeline fastened to her waist harness helped her keep both her balance and her confidence. Slowly she progressed the few feet to the dangling child.

"Now, Amy," she said when she was near enough to touch her, "listen very carefully, honey.

When I get close enough, I want you to reach out with only one arm and hold on to my shoulder. Then with the other, so that you're riding piggyback. Understand?"

Amy nodded, her eyes wide with terror.

Lucky inched closer and tried to prepare herself for the weight of the child. She clung desperately to the damp, meager handholds in the rock.

Amy scrambled onto Lucky's back like a monkey, her little fingers gripping her shoulders fiercely. Even through her sweater Lucky felt the cold dampness of the child's body. Her sobbing subsided immediately.

"That's it. You're a good, brave girl," Lucky murmured. "All set?" She felt herself teeter on the ledge, aware that the rope alone held them to the face of the bluff. She took a deep breath and felt for a toehold with her left foot and a fingerhold with her left hand.

Making every movement exaggeratedly slow and deliberate, Lucky inched back across the ledge. With the burden of the child on her back, the return trip seemed much longer. The best she could hope for was to keep from becoming a deadweight on the end of the rope, to help King and his makeshift lifeline all she could. Once more she marveled at how little communication was necessary between them. There seemed to be an intuitive link, an instinctive awareness of each other's movements, an unspoken confidence that allowed them to work together smoothly and efficiently.

Once safely across the ledge, the steep climb back to the top of the bluff seemed less formidable. She pushed away the danger of overconfidence and concentrated on finding secure footholds among the treacherously loose shale and eroding rock fragments. She ignored the pain from raw and bleeding hands gripping the rope. And every few steps she had to stop to catch her breath and shift Amy's weight. The child whimpered softly in her ear.

With the rim of the bluff in view, Lucky stumbled. She pitched forward and, to keep from plunging over the edge of the shelf into the chasm, threw her weight to the right and fell on her knees against the solid wall of the bluff. Amy screamed. Dislodged stones and soil rebounded down the slope and into the canyon.

Lucky heard King's gasp, felt the lifeline go slack momentarily before it tightened. She sagged against the rock face of the cliff. The child on her back cried in her ear, and her curls were damp against Lucky's neck. But exhaustion ate at her consciousness and waves of blackness edged out even the awareness of the mist on her face. Of all the barriers to success on this mission, the one she had most feared had indeed brought her down. The endurance of her own frail body had failed.

She felt the tug of the lifeline.

"Lucky! Just a few more feet! Come on, sweetheart, you can do it!" King's voice reached her as though from a great distance.

She pushed back to her knees and, fumbling for a handhold on the face of the cliff beside her, rose painfully to her feet. Amy shifted on her back.

"Come on, one foot in front of the other," King called, tugging on the rope. Hand over hand he was pulling now, lending his strength to hers.

With the lifeline forcing her to step or be pulled off her feet, and with King's voice urging her upward, Lucky stumbled to the rim of the bluff.

When King reached out for Amy, she screamed and clung to Lucky's neck. Lucky staggered over the edge of the cliff and collapsed to the ground. Pushing away the waves of exhaustion, she pulled the terrified youngster into her lap. "Shh, it's all right, Amy, this man is our friend." Rocking Amy to and fro, she murmured, "He helped me find you and helped us off the bluff. It's all right." She smoothed Amy's hair and cuddled her close. Disregarding professional detachment, she allowed her exultation at finding and saving the child to surface. Tears welled in her eyes and she buried her face against Amy's shoulder.

King squatted beside her. "That mean, bad man is gone, Amy. My name's King. Come sit on my lap and let Lucky rest. Okay?" His voice, soft and reassuring, coaxed the child to leave Lucky's embrace and come to him. His broad smile brought

Amy into his arms. He engulfed her with his jacket and held her close.

Lucky sprawled face down on the ground. She lay with her head on her arms, heard only her heart pounding in her ears. But after a while she became aware of King's talking softly to the child. Cosmo whined nearby, probably concerned for her and excited that the quarry for whom he had searched so long and so hard was safely at hand.

Lifting her head from her arm, Lucky looked around and saw Cosmo lashed to a nearby tree with King's belt. Even in the emergency, King had considered her regard and concern for the dog's safety.

King sat cross-legged nearby, Amy still in his lap, a first-aid kit open beside him on the ground. Tenderly he dabbed an antiseptic-soaked cotton ball onto the cuts and scrapes on Amy's arms and legs. When the child grimaced in pain, he blew gently on the wound.

"My head hurts, King." Amy passed a small hand before her eyes. "Blow here too."

As King complied, he felt Lucky's gaze and met her eyes with a smile. "Nothing too serious here. But exposure for sure, possibly shock."

Amy's face lit up when she grinned at Lucky, a spot of color in her cheeks at last.

Lucky sat up. For the first time she noticed that Amy wore a man's shirt—a dirty plaid, the sleeves tightly rolled, the hem dragging on the ground. No wonder the child had tripped on the ledge.

Amy held up the hem of the shirt as she ran into Lucky's arms. Lucky asked King, "What kind of man would kidnap a child, carry her through the woods for two days, lose her in a flooded creek, abandon her on the bluff, and yet give her the shirt off his back? For that matter, why didn't he head for the highway instead of the river?"

King shook his head. "Beats me. The world is full of strange things. I suspect this guy's not playing with a full deck. Are *you* okay?"

She nodded. "Did you raise anybody on the radio?" She dried her face and smoothed wisps of hair under her cap. "I must look a mess."

His face lit in a smile. "You've never looked more beautiful." He almost blushed, then turned his attention back to Amy. After removing his jacket to wrap around her, he fished in his pack for a down vest to replace it. "I don't know whether I got anyone, but I broadcast that we have Amy safe and sound. Maybe a slight concussion. Nothing that a bowl of hot soup and a good night's sleep won't cure, I think." He met her eyes. "I asked them to pick us up on that road near the old home place."

She said nothing but stumbled to her feet. Cosmo needed the reinforcement of greeting the child, to satisfy himself that the trail was successfully ended. Unfastening him from the tree, she gripped his harness and approached Amy.

Amy turned to the big dog and clapped her

hands. She pointed a pudgy finger. "Doggy," she said with a toothy grin.

Lucky nodded and blinked back tears. "Nice doggy. He told us where to find you."

Cosmo wriggled with delight as Amy petted his wrinkled brow and fondled his ears.

"Good dog!" Lucky said again and again, hugging him to her side and enduring his wet kisses. She wiped Amy's tear-stained face and clasped the child to her. She watched King stow the first-aid kit. "Did you mean what you said? About . . . ?"

He looked up quickly. "Yes. I love you and I'm not going to let you go again. You can be a cop in Arkansas just as well as Kansas City. And God knows we need bloodhound handlers in this neck of the woods. Last year we had a record number of lost campers and canoers."

She cleared her throat. "King, I'm going on. I'm gonna get that guy if it's the last thing I ever do."

"And it well may be," he returned immediately. "Look at you. You're exhausted. So is the dog, and footsore. Haven't you both been through enough?" He rose, squatted before her, and peered into her face. "You've accomplished your mission. You found Amy against impossible odds. You saved her life. Now let somebody else mop up."

"King, whether I like it or not, and I'm not so sure anymore that I do, I'm a police officer. A kidnapper, possibly the lowest form of criminal, is not far ahead of me. No way can I turn my back on my responsibility here." She held his gaze. "By the time those guys get around to it, he'll be long gone. You said yourself that he probably knows a way off the bluff. Once he's on the river, or holed up in another cave he knows of somewhere, they may never get him. But I'm here now and so is Cosmo. I won't take the chance of letting him get away."

He got to his feet. "It'll be dark soon." He stood by her side, and she felt his gaze on her. "What about Amy? We've got to get her to proper care."

"Of course. You'll take her out. You're strong enough to carry her and I'm not. I'm the bloodhound handler and the cop. I'll go on."

"You've got it all figured out, haven't you? What about a backup? I thought you were a better cop than to go after a desperate man with no backup."

"King, my mind is made up. I'm going on. You take Amy out and then catch up, if you want to, or call in Tank and the FBI and whoever else wants to come." She held his eyes. "But I'm going on."

He jammed his hands into the pockets of his vest and stared into the fog over the river. "All right." As he turned toward her, his eyes blazed. "And I don't doubt that you and Cosmo can find him. But have you thought about what you're going to do with him when you do? Have you considered how you can handle both the bloodhound and the kidnapper—probably in the dark as well as the rain and fog—without a backup?"

"Of course I have," Lucky said. That problem

had been gnawing at the back of her mind ever since she realized the man had abandoned Amy to the bluff. She had also worried about a scent article for the bloodhound. Given time that she didn't have, she might have located his footprint back along the trail. But the kidnapper had solved that one by giving Amy his shirt.

King looked skeptical. "Won't that just confuse Cosmo, since Amy is right here?"

"Cosmo knows she's here," Lucky replied. "He also scents another person on this shirt, one who *isn't* here. And it helps that he has also been smelling this person's scent all along this trail. He'll simply look for the one who isn't here."

While King untied the rope from Cosmo's lead, Lucky gulped a sandwich and lukewarm coffee from King's pack. Deciding it would be unwise to run the bloodhound on a full stomach, she pocketed a pouch of dog food in case there was time later to feed him.

She traded King's sweater for her warm uniform coat, then hooked the dog once more to her waist harness. His tail waving slightly, Cosmo followed her movements. She shook her head in wonder. Two days on the trail, bone-tired, footsore and hungry, the hound was still willing to work.

King watched her preparations in silence, his brow knit in a frown. "I don't see how I can let you do this," he said.

"It's not your decision." Nor was it really her

own decision, since the die was cast on the day she allowed the police department to subsidize her education.

He lowered his eyes quickly, but she saw in them a flash of the same pain she had inflicted five years ago. He shook his head and stared into the impenetrable fog over the river.

"King, do you believe in me?"

"Of course." He snatched his leather gloves from a hip pocket. "Take these, and this time I insist."

Though they were too big to be comfortable, Lucky gladly accepted the gloves. Already blistered and stiff with pain, her hands could take no more abuse. No matter what lay ahead of them, she must be able to handle Cosmo's lead.

King said, "I figure this guy might be heading for the ruins of an old, abandoned town southeast of here. Not many people left who know about it. No road goes in there anymore and hasn't for years, ever since they bought up the land for the national forest in the thirties. Just a few old lumbering shacks. The forest grew up, in, and around it fifty years ago. But if he knows this country like I think he does, he may head for it, especially if he thinks he lost us at the bluff. If I can't find you otherwise, I'll try it. In the meantime, if you stumble in there, or can get there with him, stay there. Okay?"

She nodded and returned his hug.

He stepped away from her, then stopped.

"Here." He unsnapped the radio from his belt. "You'd better take this. If it *is* getting out, you could at least radio your whereabouts and then wait for someone to pick you up. Agreed?"

"Roger." She gave him a quick smile, traded her useless radio for his, and snapped it onto her belt beside her canteen.

Realizing that her new friend was departing, Amy began to wail. She clung to Lucky's legs.

King swept the child into his arms. "Hey now, none of that." He snuggled Amy against his neck. "We must help Lucky by being brave. Come on now, you've been such a brave, big girl."

Amy's sobs quieted and she leaned to Lucky for a good-bye kiss.

"I'll see you later," Lucky said brightly as she embraced the little girl. "That's a promise," she added, meeting King's gaze. She kissed Amy's cheek, then King's.

With his free arm he pulled her against him and held her tightly. "I'll catch up as soon as I can," he vowed, his voice low and urgent. He kissed her temple. "It'll be dark soon and the fog's getting worse. Don't run over the bluff again," he murmured against her cheek.

Lucky clung to him. "Don't worry about me. Just get Amy to a warm bed." She pulled his head down and kissed him on the lips, then broke away. "I've got to go," she whispered, and twisted away from him. She leaned down to the dog with the kid-napper's shirt. "Cosmo, find!"

The bloodhound sniffed at the shirt, gave her a puzzled look, then glanced over his shoulder to Amy. The wrinkles on his brow seemed deeper and more worried than ever.

"*Find,* Cosmo!" Lucky said, holding the shirt be-fore his face.

The dog thrust his giant snout into the shirt and worked his nose, separating Amy's scent from that of an absent stranger. Head down, he circled the little group on the bluff. Satisfied that everyone was accounted for except the owner of the second, mys-terious scent in the shirt, he began to cast for the stranger's trail. His ears trailed along the ground as he swept his head from side to side.

Lucky held her breath. She and King and the lit-tle girl had milled around a large area, surely tram-pling on the scent of the kidnapper. But there was no wind to disperse the scent or blow it into the river gorge. Given time, Cosmo would sort it out. Tail drooping, he cast along the edge of the bluff.

With one eye on the cliff and one on the blood-hound, Lucky urged him on. But when, tail up, the dog found the trail and strained into the harness to follow it, he led her precariously near the rim.

"Take it easy," King called after her.

Unwilling to look away from the edge of the abyss, Lucky waved a hand in acknowledgment.

Chapter Ten

*C*osmo's tail and his relaxed manner suggested that he was trailing easily and apparently less footsore, thanks to the enforced rest. To avoid a repetition of the mad dash over the bluff, she clutched the knots in the lead. When the hound increased the pace to a lope, Lucky did not object. The sooner this nightmare trail ended, the sooner she could— do what?

What could her future, immediate and otherwise, hold? Maybe she should have quit while she was ahead. Her superiors might have overlooked her many breaches of procedure when she brought in the lost child. But to stubbornly press on after the kidnapper, blatantly ignoring all the rules, would not be so easy to forgive, especially if she failed.

She discovered that she didn't care. Her mission now was a personal one—simply to bring in the monster who had so scared little Amy.

And then what about King? She shelved the

thought for later. Now was not the time for day-dreams.

Talk about poor procedure, she thought. Over-working Cosmo when she should have had access to at least one more hound, repeatedly pressing on, improperly equipped, without essential backup—especially now, in the pursuit of a known criminal, a contaminated scent article, even letting her mind wander when she should be paying strict attention to the job at hand.

Without backup she must be especially careful to think for both herself and the hound. She watched Cosmo closely. He lowered his nose to the ground only occasionally now, and he carried his tail erect. The kidnapper's scent was good.

The trail closely followed the river bluff for per-haps a mile. She marveled at the reserves of energy in both herself and the dog. But the pumped-up adrenaline that enabled them to keep going also worked for the fugitive. With one important differ-ence. The release of his own additional adrenaline subtly increased the scent he left in his wake. Cosmo would trail him easily no matter how rug-ged the terrain.

When they struck the trace of a former road leading away from the river, Cosmo turned to the southeast. From all appearances, not even a four-wheel-drive vehicle had used this road in some time. Grass blanketed the entire roadbed and young trees homesteaded in the former tire tracks.

The forest crowded in on both sides, the branches of trees on either side nearly meeting in the middle. Here the growth was so thick that, even though still leafless, the trees formed some shelter from the drizzle. But in the depths of these woods, darkness came early, especially when abetted by the relentless fog.

Why am I taking this chance? Lucky wondered. Was she really motivated solely by the burning desire to capture Amy's kidnapper? Or was she hoping to justify her existence as a bona fide police officer after countless "easy" trails? Did she hope to prove something to her dad? To her sergeant? To King? Or even to herself?

King was right, she decided. The kidnapper would not expect to be pursued away from the bluff. He was probably unaware of the bloodhound doggedly trailing him even now. She had surprise on her side.

Other than her own muffled footfalls, little sound came from the dense forest. Occasionally a twig snapped under the weight of some wild creature, or a long-tenacious acorn plopped into the leafy humus. The old road was so overgrown that at times it was difficult to see. Or was it the foggy twilight, not yet dark but far from light? The mist had lessened, but it was growing colder. Her panting breath merged with the shifting fog.

Cosmo ran head up, nose working, his warm exhalations steaming into the air. So close were they behind him that the kidnapper's scent still lingered above the ground. They must be hard on his heels, and she began to fear they would run onto him without warning.

Suddenly a building loomed out of the fog. Lucky started, then remembered King's description of the deserted town. She shuddered. "Ghost" town would be more accurate.

She hauled in Cosmo's lead to slow him down. Common sense dictated that it would be unwise to barge into the group of buildings in the fading light. The trace of road they had been following led into their midst.

Squinting into the dusky fog, she examined each ghostly structure as they drew abreast of it. From the way the derelict buildings were arranged along the road, she guessed that it must have been the main road into town, or perhaps even the only road.

With Cosmo pulling eagerly on the lead and towing her along, she advanced cautiously into the Halloween village, the sound of her breathing audible in the silence of the forest. Each of the abandoned frame buildings, long since stripped of protective or decorative paint by time, seemed to materialize in turn as a slightly darker gray shape out of the fog. All teetered on meager corner-post foundations of piled stones, apparently without mortar of any kind. Once the stones might have supported the buildings adequately, but that was no longer true. They sagged wearily under their rusty corrugated-tin roofs, and each leaned at a different cockeyed angle.

With a guilty start, Lucky remembered her responsibility to the bloodhound, and she studied his present reaction to the kidnapper's trail of scent. Tail stiffly erect, head high, he seemed at ease on the trail. King was right. The fugitive had come to town. But was he still here?

Sliding her hand down to the next knot to shorten Cosmo's lead and the distance between them, she quickened her pace. As eager as always for her loving praise at the end of the trail, he leaned into his harness.

As she jogged along the narrow aisle between the encroaching forest and the decrepit buildings, Lucky realized that it was nearly dark, with a ghostly glow in the air. The ruins of the lumbering town loomed like tombstones.

Gradually the shape of the buildings changed slightly, and Lucky recognized the architecture of turn-of-the-century homes. Most had porches that sagged in various stages of rot, some with floorboards fallen in, others with roofs that blocked the front door. Others, remarkably untouched by time, seemed to await the return of the mistress, gone only next door to visit.

To her right, on one such porch, a pressed-back kitchen chair still beckoned invitingly. How pleasant it must have been to pass the time of evening in the cool twilight after a hard day's work in the timber. The skeleton of a picket fence, color lost, straggled around the yard and fell to ruin near its corner. There a granddaddy oak spread its branches from the eaves of the house nearly across the road. What a pleasant, shady corner it must have been.

She glanced back to Cosmo. His tail had begun to wave happily, signaling that his quarry was very close. *Forewarned is forearmed,* Lucky thought. Even if the kidnapper was not expecting her, it would not be wise to come upon him suddenly in the dusk. She slowed the eager hound to a walk and dropped the lead fastened to her belt in order to free both hands. Wincing in pain, she pulled off King's gloves and stuffed them into a coat pocket.

She unsnapped the leather flap over her service revolver and peered into the gloom. If she were going to meet the kidnapper unexpectedly in the darkening forest, she should have her pistol at the ready.

But before her gun barrel could clear the holster, the man leaped at her from behind the trunk of the giant oak. Engulfing her from the rear, he pinned her arms to her sides and clawed at her right hand, attempting to wrest the gun from her grasp.

She clung desperately to the pistol. Struggling violently, she attempted to twist against his slick, nylon-quilted jacket. But the iron grip of his arms remained secure. His bushy beard swept her neck; his hot breath was foul upon her face.

As though from a great distance Lucky heard Cosmo's frantic barking. Dragged this way and that by the force of the struggle and the lead still fastened to Lucky's waist, the dog danced beside her in an effort to keep his feet clear of the melee. Confused and frightened, trained only to trail and to save lives, the loyal and affectionate dog was capable of great concern for her safety, but he would be of no assistance in the fight against her attacker.

Unable to twist free, Lucky bent her knees, lifted her feet from the ground, and threw her weight from side to side in an attempt to break the man's hold on her. He grunted and staggered under her weight, but his grip tightened and he wrenched at the fingers of her right hand to loosen them from her revolver.

She drew her right leg up to her thigh, clenched the muscles in her leg, then jammed her foot with all her might onto the man's ankle. He cursed in surprise and pain, and quickly she repeated her attack, this time finding his instep with her heavy hiking boot. His hold on her slackened only slightly, but Lucky had seized the advantage, and she writhed against him and twisted to free her left arm. She dared not release her grip on the butt of the revolver in her right hand.

His hold on her left side slipped to her forearm. Quickly she raised her left shoulder in an attempt to catch him under the chin, but he had expected the blow and ducked it. While he waited for her next offensive move, she jerked her left arm up sharply and broke his hold on it. She knew she was fighting for her life. This man had left a baby to die, and he would not hesitate to kill her. And Cosmo.

Apparently thinking that she would snatch at his head with the free arm, the man countered by grabbing for her arm overhand in midair, thereby exposing his thick middle. Lucky bent her elbow sharply away from his grasp and, with all her strength, she bunched her biceps and drove her elbow into his stomach and chest.

The breath rushed from his body and, gasping for air, he hunched his back, drew in both hands to protect his torso, and doubled over in pain. Lucky whirled, clutched his lowered head with both hands, braced her left foot and knee, caught him under the chin with her left shoulder, and drove her right knee into his groin. Groaning a curse, he sank to his knees and collapsed to the ground before her.

Quickly she drew the revolver and slipped off the safety. "Don't move!" she ordered, extending the gun with both hands.

Without taking her eyes from the man prostrate at her feet, she said, "Cosmo, *down!*" He must not be caught in the line of fire. From the corner of her eye she saw that the hound, wild-eyed and panting heavily, was dropping obediently to the ground.

She swallowed the lump of fear in her throat. "Put your hands on top of your head and get up, very slowly." She scarcely recognized her own voice of authority.

The kidnapper stared up at her unflinchingly, his darkly glittering eyes too small for his large, ruddy face. Time seemed to stand still while he studied her intent. He had lost his quilted black hat in the struggle; his grizzled red hair, matching his unkempt beard, gave him the appearance of a wild man. He rubbed the belly of his filthy jeans with both freckled hands, then seemed to decide against challenging the gun.

But as he slowly raised his arms toward his head, there was a crashing in the underbrush. Lucky's gaze wavered only momentarily toward the dark shape emerging from the misty woods. But seizing the moment, the man before her sprang up from the ground, swinging a fallen tree branch like a club. At the same instant Cosmo leaped to his feet and shunted away from the charge, pulling Lucky off balance. Staggering sideways, she tried to level and aim the pistol while avoiding the blow.

From out of the fog, King hurtled into the clearing and threw himself between Lucky and the swinging club. He charged into the fugitive and knocked him off balance.

But the blow from the heavy tree limb glanced

off King's shoulders and head. He fell to his knees, teetered there a moment, then slumped to the ground.

Entangled in Cosmo's lead, Lucky fought for her balance. By the time she recovered, the kidnapper stood over King with his club upraised. Like a scene in a nightmare, the fog swirled around his huge form. A single sledgehammer blow would finish King.

Without taking her gaze from the criminal and his weapon, Lucky fumbled for and unfastened the hook linking her to the bloodhound. "Cosmo, down and stay!" she ordered. Loose jowls drooling saliva, the frightened dog lowered himself to the ground by her side.

She leveled the revolver at the man threatening King. "I'm a police officer," she announced icily. "Drop it or I'll shoot!"

He met her gaze with a sneer that revealed tobacco-stained teeth. His eyes flickered over her muddy uniform trousers and coat, the damp watch cap pulled low over her ears. "You don't look like no cop to me." His voice was little more than a growl. He brandished the club over King's head like a baseball bat. The trees crowded around them in the darkness and the fog softened their outlines.

Lucky steeled her voice. "Make no mistake. I'll drop you where you stand if you don't throw down that branch. I'll show you my credentials and read you your rights later—if you live long enough."

For a long moment the kidnapper stared, his pig-like eyes mere slits in his round face. Lucky sensed that he was weighing the possibility of a woman cop so deep in the national forest. Or was testing her nerve.

She cocked the gun and held his eyes without wavering. "Drop it!"

Finally, while her heart beat violently, he tossed away the branch and lifted his hands to the top of his bushy head. Without taking her gaze from him, Lucky fumbled at the back of her belt for her handcuffs. She had not used them since her training days at the academy, and now she wondered if she could operate them. Her hands, so stiff and sore, might present another problem.

But the kidnapper offered no further resistance. She handcuffed him to a nearby sapling in a sitting position.

"Okay, good dog, Cosmo!" She released the hound from his down-stay and petted him briefly. Later she would give him the praise and reward he deserved for this day's work. But now, mindful of King's injury, she hurried to him and knelt by his side, the dog at her heels.

Half carrying and half dragging him, Lucky supported King's effort to move to the giant oak. Determined to sit upright, he sprawled against the tree and fought for consciousness. Blood oozed from a gash on his forehead, and an eye had begun to swell shut.

Cosmo whimpered and crowded close to King, pushing at him with his nose. When King failed to rise, he settled down beside him, his head on King's thigh.

Lucky sighed, wondering if there was anything in her sergeant's ever-handy book of regulations about the proper procedure for simultaneously retrieving a fugitive, an injured man, and an exhausted, footsore hound from a fog-shrouded mountain single-handedly in the darkness.

Unsnapping the canteen from her belt, she dampened her handkerchief and, ignoring the sting of the water on her raw hands, she bathed King's face.

He smiled up at her. Catching one of her hands, he raised it to his lips. "Remind me to buy a fistful of tickets to the policewomen's ball," he murmured with a grin.

She returned his smile and leaned to kiss his forehead. "What did you do with Amy?"

"I got so worried about you I couldn't think, but it finally dawned on me that I had only to take her down the bluff to some people I know who live on the river below there." He squeezed her hand. "Don't worry. She's fine. But to be on the safe side, they were going to call an ambulance. They'll let Tank and her folks know she's okay, then send somebody up here after us."

Lucky sagged against the tree trunk and slid down it to sit beside him. Linking her arm through his, she exulted in the realization that she no longer had to prove anything to anybody. Nor, for that matter, to herself. She had honored her debt to Dad and to the police force with five years of her youth. The rest belonged to her and to King.

Cosmo snuggled closer to King's leg and heaved a sigh, as if thankful that Lucky would at last rest. In a moment he was snoring noisily, his jowls fluttering with every exhalation of breath. King rested a hand on the dog's back.

Leaning her head on King's shoulder, Lucky decided it would be reassuring to have a permanent backup, to be part of a team. No longer must she feel the need to face the world alone.

"Well, you were wrong about one thing," she murmured. "I can't be a cop just as well in Arkansas as I can in Kansas City."

She felt him stiffen slightly, but he said nothing.

"In fact, I can't be a cop any easier in Arkansas now than I could have been five years ago."

He took a deep breath as though to speak, but she cut him off. "But I've learned that a cop's life isn't really for me. I don't like dealing with endless paperwork, preposterous budgets, handcuffs and guns." She snuggled against him. "What I like—and what I really want to do—is to live in Arkansas where I belong, and to work bloodhounds. And train them. I want to have a houseful of little girls like Amy and to train a never-ending supply of

Cosmos and Moonshines to find toddlers lost in the woods, and also old ladies and gentlemen."

King slipped an arm around her and pulled her close. "And could your friendly forest ranger convince you to organize and head up a local search-and-rescue squad?"

She pretended to consider. "Mmm, I don't know."

She felt his smile in the darkness. "I can guarantee plenty of local respect and affection for the wife of the friendly forest ranger," he said.

She nodded. "Well, in that case. . . ."